DOC STEEL

Published by DL Gallie Author

First published 18th December 2019 as part of the Dirty Dozen, Alpha Edition anthology

Second edition, 21st April 2020

Cover designed by **Stacey Blake**, Champagne Book Design

Edited by **Karen Hrdlicka**, Barren Acres Editing

Formatting and interior design by **DL Gallie**

Returning to civilian life isn't easy for Griffin Steel, that is,
until he runs into Autumn White.
She's stunning, vivacious, and has that same spark he fell for
twenty years ago. Until he ripped her heart out and took it
with him when he enlisted.
Picking up the remains of her shattered soul, Autumn found
love again, and life was great for a while.

Until it wasn't.

Now she's a single mom, finally getting her life together, and
the last thing she expects is to run into the man who still
holds a major piece of her heart.
The temptation is too strong as all those feelings Autumn had
for Griffin, flare back to life.

It's inevitable.
Magnetic.
Explosive.

Everything they have been missing for the past twenty years,
and more.

It's perfect.

Until the father of her child returns.
He will stop at nothing to reclaim Autumn and his son as
his own.

A NOTE FROM THE AUTHOR

Doc Steel originally approved in the Dirty Dozen:Alpha edition anthology.
Its the same sexy story but now has its own sexy as sin cover.

ALSO BY DL GALLIE

STAND ALONES

Out of Nowhere

Antecedent

Seven Nights

Falling for Dr. Kelly, a Falling novel

Falling for Dr. Knight, a Falling novel - preorder now

The Rule Breaker anthology

THE CASTAWAY GROVE COLLECTION

Love has arrived in the Grove

Oasis

Unequivocal Love

Five Words

...and a few more as well.

THE LIQUOR CABINET SERIES

Liquor has never been so disturbingly saucy

Malt Me (Book 1)

Tequila Healing (Book 2)

Wine Not (Book 3)

The Final Shot (Book 4)

The Liquor Cabinet: Series boxset

THE UNEXPECTED SERIES

When it comes to love, expect the unexpected

The Unexpected Gift

The Unexpected Letter

The Unexpected Package

The Unexpected Connection

PROLOGUE

...Twenty years earlier

"ARE YOU FREAKIN KIDDING ME, GRIFF?" SHE shouts, her voice laced with anger, shock, and sadness. "You accept this without talking to me first?" This is not how I expected her to react. I expected excitement and happiness. Not like this.

The 'this' Autumn is referring to is I just joined the navy and entered into their medical training program. I was amazed at what they offered in regard to the training and immediately signed up. Sure, I was shocked I enlisted, it was never on my radar, but it was too good of an offer to pass up. Not only will my degree be covered by the government but they will also pay me so study. I was so excited; I accepted immediately and couldn't wait to tell Autumn the news. This will be a huge financial relief for us; the only downfall is I need to move to Portsmouth, Virginia. I was sure Autumn would be happy and excited for me. For us. I certainly didn't think she'd react like this.

"I thought I was doing the right thing," I plead, "My degree will be paid for, sure I have to serve, but in the long run, it will be great for us."

"No, Griff, it will be great for you. While you are off sailing the high seas, I'll be here. Alone." She wipes her eyes, which are now glassy with tears. "I can't believe you are going to walk away from us."

"I'm not walking away from us. I'm doing this for us. Don't you see?"

She stares at me, the first tear falls and she angrily wipes it away. "No, this is all for you."

With those words, she turns and walks away from me. Racing over to her, I grab her hand and spin her to face me. We stare at one another. Her eyes well with tears and she begins to sob uncontrollably. Lifting my hand, I wipe away her tears. Bending down, I rest my forehead against her. "Autumn, I promise this will all work out. I need you to trust me."

"I do trust you, but I just don't see how you being a million miles away will work." She swallows back a sob, "Please don't do this."

"I'm sorry, I have to."

She sighs deeply, I can finally see acceptance whirring around in her face. "When do you leave?"

My lips lift in a smile, I knew she'd come around. "In two weeks."

"What?" she screeches. "I thought we'd have more time."

"I know, me too, but now you see why I had to make this decision as quickly as I did."

She nods. "I understand," she mumbles but really she doesn't, she just said that to appease me.

"I love you, Autumn," I vow, placing a kiss on her forehead.

"I love you too, forever and eternity," she whispers back to me.

Forever and eternity, that's what we always said to one another, and I really hope that our love mantra is true.

The next two weeks, all we do is fight and bicker about anything and everything. I try everything to get her to see this is great for us. I even try to get her to come with me. She doesn't want to leave Sandpoint, it is her home. Her family and friends are here. I want her to be happy, so I stopped asking her to move with me. After a long discussion, we agree to stay together but I know we won't, there is too much hurt in her heart.

The morning I leave, she is cold and distant. I know I've already lost her. On one hand I am excited for the venture ahead, but on the other, I am losing the one I love unconditionally. We kiss goodbye but there is no passion in it, it is robotic. She stands there and watches as I walk toward the plane. The plane taking me to Portsmouth, Virginia, where I will one day become Doctor Griffin Steel.

At the top of the stairs, I look back at her and my heart broke. She is crouched down, staring at the plane, tears streaming down her face. And I know: those tears and her heartbreak are because of me. In that moment, I start to wonder if maybe I'm making a mistake...career-wise, it is the best decision I ever made. In regard to Autumn; it is a huge mistake.

...Present day

TODAY IS THE FIRST DAY OF THE REST OF MY LIFE, OR so they tell me. To me, it's the first day in hell. The navy is—no WAS my life—and for the past twenty years, I knew what I was doing on a daily basis. Now? I'm free to do what I want, when I want...but I don't know what I want.

Returning to Sandpoint, Idaho wasn't what I wanted to do, but with Mom's recent passing, Dad needed me. The timing was perfect, well as perfect as the death of your mother can be. Seeing Dad so heartbroken over Mom's death is hard to deal with. She was his everything and when she died, a piece of him died too. Him wanting me to return here is the least I could do. So, after her funeral, I returned to Portsmouth where I handed in my retirement paperwork—something I didn't expect to do so soon in my navy career. Then I packed everything up, and moved back to beautiful Sandpoint, Idaho. The place where I grew up. My childhood here was great, it was also where I let the best thing that ever happened to me go, Autumn White. I often wonder what she's up to; where she ended up. Wherever she is, I hope she's happy.

With my coffee in hand, I take a sip and the caffeine goodness warms my soul. With a newfound smile on my face—thank you, coffee—I step out of the coffee shop and a little boy runs into my legs. He falls onto his butt with a thud. Dropping down to his height, I stretch out my hand to him. "You okay, little dude?"

His eyes widen and he stares at me open-mouthed as I pull him into a standing position. His mother comes running along, "Oliver James White, what have I told you about running off?"

Now it's my turn for my eyes to bug wide open. I'd recognize that voice anywhere, and when I lift my gaze from the little boy in front of me, my ears were correct. Autumn White is walking, no stalking, toward me, and she is just as stunning now as she was twenty years ago when I left, if anything she has gotten sexier with age.

She stops midstep when her eyes land on me. Recognition flares and her baby blue orbs pop open in shock. Her mouth drops open and closes a few times, but nothing comes out. She stops next to who I assume is her son, her eyes still locked on me. From my crouched position with the little boy, I crane my neck to look at her. I smile but she doesn't return one. Standing back up, we continue to stare at one another, neither of us saying a thing. Just like it used to, the air crackles around us.

Everything but her fades into the background. The silence is broken when a small voice says, "I'm sorry, Mom." He steps to her and hugs her sideways.

Her gaze drops to the little boy. "You need to be more careful. You could have hurt Commander Steel." She places emphasis on the word Commander, guess she's still not impressed that I enlisted and left.

"Just plain old Doc Steel now, I'm retired."

Her eyes bug open again, "You...you're back for good then?"

Nodding my head, I don't say anything but my eyes roam over her. She's still petite but her breasts have gotten bigger. Her legs are still sexy as hell. That dimple on her left cheek is more prominent now and her eyes are as blue as ever; she's just how I remember her but sexier.

The voice of the little boy, snaps my attention down to him. "I'm sorry, Commander Steel. I was just so excited." His voice raising at the last part.

Dropping back to his height, I smile. "And why are you excited today?"

"Momma is letting me have a muffin AND a milkshake."

"You must have done something really good to get a treat like that."

He nods his head. "Yep, I slept through the night for three whole nights."

"Way to go, little man." The pride on his face and in his voice is remarkable. Offering up my hand for a high-five, his little hands slaps mine. I pretend it hurts and shake my hand back and forth. "You've got a good left hook there, buddy."

"Actually, Commander Steel, it was my right hand." He lifts his left hand and makes an L shape. "See, L for left."

"I'll have to remember that," I say with a smile, "You're quite clever, aren't you?"

"Yep," he proudly says. "Momma, can Commander Steel come with us?"

Her eyes pop wide open, her mouth drops but she remains silent. Giving her a reprieve, I shake my head. "Thanks for the offer, but I already have my coffee." I lift my cup to show him, "Plus, I need to go meet with Doc Miller about possibly working with him."

"You're a doctor?"

"Sure am."

"I thought you were a commander?"

"I was a doctor in the navy and I had the rank of commander."

"Wow, that's so cool." He beams. "Can I call you Commander Doc Steel?"

I don't get to answer because Autumn grabs his hand and pulls him away from me. "Come on, Ollie, it's time for your treat." She looks at me. "Goodbye, Griffin." She called me Griffin, she only ever did that when she was angry. It seems time hasn't eased the pain I caused. Before I can say anything, she turns and walks away from me. Her dismissal and retreat sting, I guess this is what she felt all those years ago when I left.

I stare at the door of the coffee shop as that day flits through my mind. Shaking away the memory of the day I broke her heart, I turn and walk toward the Doc Miller's office. I had hoped time would have healed the wound I left on her heart, and maybe, I'd get a second chance with her. After seeing her just now, it won't be easy to win her over. Then again, she does have a kid now, and I bet Mr. Autumn dotes on her like the queen she is. *Lucky bastard.*

Looking over, I see her staring at me through the coffee shop window. She smiles shyly at me, I know from the look in her eyes she's remembering our past too. Maybe she'd settle for friendship, but can I be just friends with her? Guess time will tell.

TODAY IS THE FIRST DAY IN A LONG TIME THAT I CAN breathe easily. I haven't felt this at peace in a long time, not since...no, I will not dwell on the past. My life's focus now is on raising Ollie and giving him my everything. He *is* my everything and the only good thing to come from my time with Avon.

Avon Best was perfect, until he wasn't. It took me far too long to remove my rose-colored glasses, and now that I have, I will never put them back on again. For Ollie, I will do it. I need to stay strong for him, and for me.

Bumping into Griffin today was a shock. I haven't seen him in twenty years. The last time I saw him, he was leaving to start his degree and enlistment. He broke my heart leaving and I was broken, until I met Avon...and then Avon broke me and that was worse than Griffin shattering my heart. Avon broke me: mind, body, and soul. I vowed never to let a man break me again, to never let a man get under my skin and consume me. That was going well, until Ollie ran into Griffin. He has been at the forefront of my mind all day. Memories from our past keep playing on a loop in my head; we had so many good times, until we didn't. That seems to be a trend with me and the opposite sex.

The hurt I experienced all those years ago when he left is still there, but there's also the love I had for him. He was my first love, my first heartbreak. My first everything. I wonder if we will finally get our happily ever after. That sizzle between us is still there. When my eyes landed on him, my heart skipped a beat. He's just as sexy today as he was back then. If anything, age has added to his appeal. Broad shoulders. Eyes that still set my skin on fire. Rough hands that know every inch of my body. Just thinking about him and his hands has my insides quivering. Closing my eyes, my mind drifts back to a happy time with Griff and I...

...Griff and I are spending the day at the lake. He stopped to pick me up a few moments ago, and when I walk down the stairs, I feel his gaze roam over my body. I'm wearing a red and black bikini, underneath a sheer sundress, and on my feet are my flip-flops with a jewel on the side. My sunglasses cover my eyes and on my head is a floppy hat. Opening the door to his black Bronco, I climb in. Dropping my bag on the floor, I turn to him and smile. "Hi, boyfriend."

"Hi, girlfriend," he says, as he leans toward me and presses his lips to mine. My eyes drop closed and I thread

my fingers around his neck, pulling him closer to me. He breaks our kiss and rests his forehead against mine. "I love kissing you."

"I love kissing you too," I whisper back, pressing my lips to his once again. I moan into his mouth when he slides his hand around my waist, pulling me closer to him. My breasts press against his chest, the friction causing my nipples to harden and my clit to throb. We have yet to take our relationship that far, but I think it's time.

"Griff," I whisper, "I think I'm ready."

He pulls back and stares at me. "What?"

"I'm ready. Tonight is the night."

"Are you sure?"

Nodding my head up and down, I smile. "Definitely sure. If it wasn't hotter than Hades out there, I'd say take me to your place and do me now, but I want our first time to be special. Tonight, I will cook us dinner, and then after dinner, I want you to make love to me until the wee hours of the morning."

"Shit, babe, you can't say that to me. Look." He points to his groin and I see that he's hard.

Leaning over, I whisper, "If you're lucky, I might help you out with that while we are swimming."

"You little minx." He kisses my nose and winks at me. "Let's go." He puts the Bronco into gear and we head toward the lake. We spent the day at the lake frolicking and making out. When the sun started to dip, we headed back to Griffin's place where the fun continued well into the wee hours of the morning.

The day was absolutely perfect, and the night, unforgettable. One I will remember forever.

. . .

Sitting on the sofa, I smile at the memory, and yes, it is one I remember forever. Every detail of the day is clear and vivid in my mind. Things with Griff and I were amazing, beyond amazing. He was my everything and I was his. We were perfect together...and then we weren't. It all changed in an instant, and from that point on, everything in my life seemed to follow that path too. Perfect one minute, imploding the next. I won't go there again, I can't let myself get hurt because Ollie needs me. I need to be the best mom for him, and I intend to do that. My heart and desires need be ignored, and they will be...for now.

My meeting with Doc Miller went well, actually it went really fucking well. He is looking to retire soon, and if all goes to plan, he's going to sell me his practice when the time comes. That's better than I could have expected. When I first called him, he didn't seem interested, but now it seems it's all falling into place. Maybe moving back to Sandpoint won't be as bad as I originally thought it would be.

With my job sorted and living arrangements almost finalized, life out of the navy isn't as overwhelming as I thought. Tonight, I'm meeting up with a few buddies who still live here for drinks. When I walk into The Tavern, I smile. This place hasn't changed since the first time I snuck in here when I was a teenager.

Jimmy Jones is behind the bar and he hasn't aged a day. "Jimmy Jones, how the hell are you?" I say, as I take a seat at the bar.

"Good, good," he says, stretching his hand across for me to shake, "Commander Steel, heard you were back."

"It's just Mr. Steel now. Actually no, that's my father, call me Griff."

"Okay, Doc it is then."

Smartass bastard. He slides a beer over to me and I pick up the mug. "Thanks." Bringing it to my lips I take a sip, the yeasty goodness of the crisp lager is just what I need. "So, what's new?"

"Same old, same old," he says, and before I can ask another question, he serves another patron. Grabbing my beer, I spin around and my eyes take in the place. It's exactly as I remember. Booths line the wall to the left as you walk in, the bar runs the length of the place on the right. The kitchen is in the right back corner, across from that a poolroom, and down the corridor between the two are the offices and restrooms. The lighting is dark, but it works, and the wood floors are just as shiny as they were the last time I was here.

Like the three musketeers that they are; James, Jamie, and Jason arrive at the same time and saunter toward me. "Well, well, well," Jason singsongs, "look who's returned home."

"Jason, good to see you, man." Standing up, I shake his hand and he pulls me in for the one-armed bro hug. Turning to James and Jamie, we greet each other in the same manner.

"Well, shit me," Old Man Johnson, James's dad, says, "the four of you back together again can only spell trouble." He pauses. "At least your ringleader has settled down and won't be here to lead you all astray." Just like that, my mind drifts to Autumn. Back in high school, the five of us used to get into so much mischief. Thankfully, we had her on our team to bat her eyelashes and get us out of the shit we found ourselves in. Without her, the four of us would have been arrested, or beaten up, on numerous occasions. Everyone knew she was the ringleader, but she had a way of making you see what she wanted.

"You seen her yet, dude?" Jamie asks me as we head toward the pool tables.

Nodding my head, I take a swig of beer. "Yep, ran into her and her son yesterday."

The three of them nod, the silence is odd, especially since my friends are anything but quiet. "Am I missing something?"

They all shake their heads no.

"Just..."

"Just what, James?"

"Just don't go all gung ho, bull in a china shop like you always do when it comes to her. She's been through a lot. She's happy, finally."

"I can see she's happy. She's got a kid and husband, I only ever wanted her to be happy."

A look passes between them. "Seriously, what am I missing here?" I ask, as I rack up the balls.

"What do know about her after you left?" James asks, he leans against the pool table and crosses his arms across his chest.

"Not much. We broke up soon after I left. When I came back before I deployed, she was gone. I hadn't seen her until I bumped into her the other day."

The three of them share a look again. "Seems I'm out in the cold and missing something. What is it?"

"Look," James says, "She's had it rough in the past. Ollie's dad is a asshole."

"Asshole is putting it lightly," Jamie adds.

"Let's just say, if he was on fire, I'd throw gasoline at him."

"Okay, baby daddy is an ass. What else is there?"

James sighs, "When she returned to Sandpoint, she was pregnant with Ollie." He pauses. "She was also black and blue with many broken bones."

My eyes snap open. "What do you mean?" I growl, my blood boiling at the thought of anyone laying their hands on Autumn.

"He'd been beating her for years. Apparently he was abusive, verbally and physically. When he found out she was pregnant, he was over the moon at first. With all the morning sickness and the focus being on her, he lost his shit and beat her pretty bad one day, and that was the day she decided to get out. Carla and Howard raced to Georgetown and brought her back here."

"Where's this fucker now?"

"Locked away. Autumn pressed charges. He pled guilty and was sentenced to seven years."

"Fuck me," I whisper.

James nods. "Dude, I've never seen her as broken as she was when she returned. But in typical Autumn style, she stepped up and was strong, for Ollie. She'd do anything for that kid, we all would." He smiles, "I was there the day she went into labor with him."

"Hence, James as his middle name." He scrunches his

eyes in confusion at me knowing this. "Ollie bumped into me after running off, she shouted his full name in anger."

"Yeah, she still does that, even to me." I laugh. That was her thing when we were younger, seems some things don't change. He looks at me. "Dude, what are you going to do?"

"What do you mean?"

"Autumn, she's been through a lot, man. I don't want to see her get hurt...again."

His statement is like a punch to the gut. "To be honest, I don't know, but I will promise you this. Whatever happens, I will not hurt her."

"Good, 'cause I'd hate to have to kick your ass."

"I'd like to see you try."

And just like that, the heaviness of our conversation dissipates and we fall into our old pattern. Playing pool and talking shit to one another.

After spending the night with the guys, I head home around midnight, but I'm too wired to sleep, my brain is firing on all cylinders. Everything I learned tonight is whirring around in my head. I'm sitting on my sofa, with a beer in hand, and all I can think about is her; the one that got away. The one I never stopped thinking about. Ever since I bumped into her and Ollie, I haven't been able to get Autumn off my mind. After hearing how her life turned out, I feel even shittier about leaving her all those years ago.

Taking another sip of beer, I wonder if maybe this is my second chance with her, not that I deserve one. She seems to still harbor a little, okay a shitton of anger toward me. I would have thought, after twenty years, she'd have let it go. But I guess with what I, and that asshat, did to her, she's hesitant when it comes to the opposite sex. But I know she still feels what I feel, I saw the look in her eyes when she saw me. The hunger, the desire, it's exactly what I feel. That spark. That connection between us is still there. I want a second chance with her, and I'm determined to mend her broken heart and give her the happily ever after she deserves.

THE RETURN OF COMMANDER STEEL IS THE TALK OF the town at the moment. Ever since I bumped into him over a week ago, he's all I hear about...all I dream and think about—*damn him*. If the lady at the store mentions he's single, one more time; I will lose my shit. Heaven forbid that two people who live in the same town are single. Never mind the fact he broke my heart. I know technically, I was the one to officially end things between us, but if he hadn't left, my heart would have been fine.

My heart just couldn't take the distance. I was lonely without Griff here. Everything reminded me of him, of all the good times we had. I hated life, actually, I hated everything, but most of all, I hated him for leaving me. Cutting ties with him and getting out of Sandpoint were the only things I could do to move on, and it worked. I enrolled to become a teacher at Indiana State University. I completed my degree and became a teacher. After graduation I secured a job in Georgetown and moved there. I loved my job working at the elementary school. Working with kids, molding them, it's so rewarding.

A few years after I moved to Georgetown was when I met Avon. I was reluctant to start anything with him, but he was persistent. After giving in, he took me on a date and I didn't hate it. He took me on a few more and I started to fall for him, I thought I'd won the lottery. Even though I loved him with everything I had, Griffin Steel still held a piece of my heart, and I think he always will. A few months after we officially started dating, we moved in together. It was perfect, my life was perfect once again, and I was ecstatically happy. I had a great job, a loving boyfriend, and great friends. I was hoping he'd propose, then we'd get married and live happily ever after. Instead, he turned into a nightmare. One minute he was the loving Avon I fell in love with, the next he was a mean bastard. It started off with a verbal insult here and there. Then the odd slap on the face. The first day he viciously assaulted me, I thought I was going to die. I'd never felt pain like I did that day, his boot in my ribs was nothing compared to him stomping on my legs. How I managed to cover up what he did that day still amazes me. I don't know how I managed to hide my injuries from that incident, but I did. How I managed to cover them up for the weeks, months, and years following I have no idea; guess I'm a good actress after all.

When I got pregnant for the second time, I thought Avon would be over the moon, going by his reaction when I lost the first one, I hoped this would be the turning point for him and us. Ohh how I was wrong. He was loving and wonderful at first, but then it all turned horrific. He savagely beat me that day, never before had he been this violent. My body was black and blue, multiple bones were broken, and that was the first time I lost consciousness after one of his attacks. Miraculously, I didn't lose the baby, but that beating opened my eyes to the way I was living, and it was the day I escaped. I called Mom and Dad and they came to my rescue. Dad pushed me to press charges against him, and I'm glad I made the decision to so. He didn't deserve to get away scot-free for what he did to me, and no woman should have to go through what I did at his hands. To this day, I still don't understand why I stayed; love makes you do stupid things, I guess.

My cousin, Jamie, put his law degree to good use and represented me. Avon was charged with assault causing bodily harm and sentenced to prison for seven years. I was relieved he was locked away, but at the same time, I was sad my baby would grow up without a dad; pregnancy hormones sure do a number to your rational thinking, well I should say lack of thinking.

After the trial, I moved back to Sandpoint and in with Mom and Dad. Once I was back on my feet, I moved into a cottage of my own and that is now where Ollie and I call home.

"Can we go to the doctor's, Mom?" Ollie pipes up, my eyes snap to his with concern at his request.

"Why? What's wrong, baby?"

"Nothing, I just want to see Doc Steel. He's so cool."

Fucking Doc Steel.

"Unless you are sick, we will not be going to the

doctor's office but we can go to Little League. Nana and Grumpy"—our playful term for Daddy since he is the least grumpy person around—"are going to meet us there." My mom and dad dote on Ollie, he is the apple of their eyes and would do anything for him and me.

With him distracted, he runs into his room; a few moments later he returns in his uniform with his mitt tucked under his arm. "Ready, let's go."

"Have you brushed your teeth?"

He frowns. "Yeeees," he innocently says.

"Nice try, buddy. Give me your mitt and go brush them and then we can go."

"Fine," he huffs.

Thirty minutes later, I'm in the stands with the other parents. Mom and Dad are running late. I'm checking my e-mail when I overhear a conversation. "Have you seen the new doc in town?"

"That's Griffin Steel," Suzi 'I'm a skank' Jones says. "He grew up here. Ex-navy. I was a few grades below him, he was hot back then, but now..." She fans herself. "I look forward to when I run into him, I'll show him my appreciation for his service." They all giggle.

"I can't wait to get sick," another one pipes up and I scoff to myself. It must be louder than I anticipated because three heads turn to face me. Thankfully Mom and Dad arrive and I'm spared the wrath from skanky Suzi.

Ollie's team wins and to celebrate the team heads to Jack in the Box, which has become tradition after a win. The kids are all eating, and us moms are at the next table chatting. When the door opens, the hairs on the back of my neck prickle and I know; he's here. Glancing over my shoulder, my eyes land on him and I stop breathing. Griffin looks like sex on a stick; he's wearing navy blue cargo shorts and a white wifebeater that accentuates his chest and arm muscles. As usual, aviators cover his eyes. Peeking across his chest is a tattoo, but from here I can't read what it says.

"Doc!" Ollie shouts and races over to him. He's beaming at the man before him and Griffin returns Ollie's smile. The two of them chatting excitedly.

The moms turn to me and their faces all say, 'How does your son know him?' "Ollie," I holler, "sit down and leave Griffin be."

"I don't mind, Autumn," he says, his voice husky and doing things to my body that I don't want to happen. How can I despise the man as much as I do, but at the same time want him to ravage me? *Whoa, where did that thought come from?* Thankfully, I'm pulled out of my head when Billy, a kid on Ollie's team, throws up.

Our time at Jack in the Box comes to an abrupt end. We pack up and leave. As I'm climbing into my car, I notice Griffin walking to his. He stops midstep and stares at me. My tongue darts out, licking my bottom lip before I bite down on it. Griffin mimics what I did, and my mind drifts to other things that I remember he can do with that tongue...

...The door to his bedroom isn't even closed yet, and Griffin is already lifting my cover-up over my head. His eyes rake over my body, heating my skin. He steps to me,

wrapping his arms around my waist. Leaning down, he licks across my collarbone. My head drops back elongating my neck; he runs his tongue up my neck to my ear. Nibbling my earlobe he huskily whispers, "Get on the bed Autumn and spread your legs for me."

He gently pushes me back and I fall to the mattress. My blonde hair fans out behind me. Lifting my head, I undo the tie of my bikini top and flick it to the floor. My eyes are locked on his, he swallows deeply as I begin to undo the tie on the side of my bikini bottom. He shakes his head at me as he drops to his knees. Grabbing my ankles, he pulls me to the edge of the bed. With his eyes locked on mine, he leans forward; flattening his tongue, he licks along my groin, breathing in my scent. "Fuck, Autumn, I love how you smell." With his tongue, he nudges the material to the side and flicks the tip of his tongue across my throbbing clit.

"Mmmmm," I moan. Gripping his head, I press him farther into me. My bikini bottom is caught in my slit, the material rubbing all the right spots as his tongue laps at my mound. "More," I groan, "I need more."

He slides his thumb into the sides of my bottoms and pulls them down my legs. Dropping the material to the floor, he leans forward and plunges his tongue into me. "Griffin," I moan as he continues to lick and fuck me with his tongue. He sucks my clit into his mouth, gently biting down. The nip is what I need and I explode around his tongue. He licks and sucks every last drop of my climax...

A car horn beeping snaps me back to the present. Griffin

steps out of the car's path and heads to his truck. I climb in, shaking my head at the memory that just surfaced, along with a pulsating throb between my legs. I start my car and pull out. Passing Griffin, he winks at me and my clit throbs harder. Even though he broke my heart, he clearly still has a pull on my body.

I'VE JUST CLOSED UP THE PRACTICE AND AM HEADING over to the cafe to grab some dinner, when I spot Autumn walking down the street with her mom and Ollie. Stopping in their path, she eyes me but I look to her mom and smile. "Mrs. White, it's so good to see you." Leaning over I kiss her cheek.

"Griffin, it's so good to see you too. I'd heard you were back. And please, call me Carla. " She glances to Autumn and they share a look.

"You've always been Mrs. White to me, it will be hard, but I will try...Carla."

She winks at me. "How's your dad?"

"Dad's doing okay. He's on a cruise at the moment, should be home next week, I think."

"Ohh, how nice. John deserves that a treat after losing your mom."

"Yeah he does, but a cruise? I bet he's loving being

trapped on a boat with four hundred strangers," I joke.

"You'd be surprised," Autumn interrupts. "He's changed." She says this with a tone that insinuates I don't know my father like she does.

We fall silent. Autumn and I stare at one another, once again the air sizzling but this time, it's not sexual, it's zinging with anger. The intenseness of the moment is broken when Ollie says, "Hey, Doc." Looking down to him, I see him grinning at me. His smile reminds me so much of his mother's, I find myself grinning back at him.

"Hey, buddy," I offer, as I ruffle his hair. "How's it going?"

"Good. Nana and Mom just took me to the park and now we are going to get pizza for dinner and watch a movie."

"Sounds like a great night." My gaze lifts to Autumn. "Autumn, you look gorgeous."

Still staring at me, her cheeks darken at my compliment. I used to love making her squirm when we were together. "Griffin," she tersely replies, eyeing me with contempt.

"I'm going to take Ollie to get ice cream for after the movie," Carla says. She takes Ollie's hand. "It was lovely to see you, Griffin." She turns and walks off, leaving me alone with Autumn.

I stare at her and she's still scowling at me. "Have I done something wrong?" She eyes me. "Other than breathing."

She laughs and shakes her head. "Ever since you returned, all I hear is Griffin fucking Steel this. Griff that. Doc Steel is so great. He's so wonderful, the service he gave our country, blah, blah, blah. Don't get me wrong, I love that you served and protected our country but..." she swallows deeply and lifts her gaze to me. "You broke me, Griffin. You were my life, you were my everything, and you left me behind. They say time heals all wounds, but when it's your heart, that's a different story."

"Autumn—"

"No," she raises her hand, "you don't get to say anything. I've bottled this up for twenty years now. The wound on my heart is just as raw today as it was back then. Your one decision changed my entire life. When you left, my life went into a downward spiral, and at one point it imploded in a way I never imagined."

"What do you mean?"

"I finally put myself out there and met someone. I was hesitant at first, the heartbreak you caused was still fresh, even though it happened years earlier. I knew I had to move on, and Avon," I shudder hearing his name pass through her lips, "was so sweet and patient. Again, I gave my heart to a man, but this time—he didn't just stomp on my heart—he also stomped on me. Figuratively and liter-ally." My eyes widen at how blasé she seems about him and what he did. When the guys told me what he did to her, I was fuming. If the fucker wasn't locked away, I wouldn't be held accountable for what I did to him. You never, never raise your hand to a women and especially not when that woman is Autumn White. She sniffs and that snaps my attention back to her. "The only good thing to come from that man was my son. Ollie is my every-thing now. I can't and will not let anything break me again." She wipes away a stray tear. "I just can't."

Before I can say anything, she's running away from me. She's gone. I'm standing here, watching her retreating form, and my blood is boiling. Autumn was always so strong and knowing what she's been through kills me. Any other person would be a mess, but not Autumn. She rose up from what happened and went on with life, raising her son alone. That makes her the strongest person I know. Her strength is one of her sexiest qualities, but underneath her strength is a broken woman, and I'm a cause of some of those cracks. As I watch her catch up to Ollie and Carla, I decide I'm going to repair what I broke. I'm going to win back the only girl I have ever loved. The heart I broke all those years ago is going to be fixed, and I'm the glue that will hold it together.

Autumn White is going to get her happily ever after and there's nothing I won't do to fix what I originally cracked.

That night as I lay in bed, I played my conversation with Autumn from earlier over and over in my head. If I had known that enlisting would have done this to the most amazing human to ever have roamed this earth, then I wouldn't have. Who knew my decision would have such dire consequences for Autumn? I would have accepted the financial burden that medical school would have rung up, Autumn would have been worth every cent.

I'm not going to give up.

Autumn White is my one and only.

I just need her to open her heart and give me another chance...and I know exactly who will help me win her over.

I can't believe I told him all of that. I can't believe I spelled out my life with Avon to him. I knew after chatting with Jason that the guys spilled some of the beans. As I was standing in front of him earlier, my mouth opened and it all came out. He looked shocked at hearing it come from me, and so he should. That was the worst time of my life. I thought after Griffin left me that would be the only soul crushing moment in my life, ohh how I was wrong. I went through a phase of blaming Griffin for Avon coming into my life. If he hadn't have left, he and I would have been happy and I never would have ended up in Georgetown, but then again, Griff and I could have split up and I still could have ended up there. You cannot live your life with what-ifs, you can only learn from your mistakes and what life throws at you. I've learned the only person you can rely on is yourself and since I discovered this, I haven't let myself down.

"Mom!" Ollie shouts as he races into my bedroom, launching himself though the air up onto the bed next to me.

"What have I told you about jumping on beds?"

"Sorry, Mom." He smiles at me and my heart fills with joy. Ollie is my everything and he has me wrapped around his little finger. He manages to sweet talk everyone he meets. "I need to go to the doctor's."

His words startle me. "Why baby? What's wrong?" I reach out and pull him to me. I feel his forehead for a temperature but he's fine.

"Nothing's wrong, Mom. I just want to see Doc Steel."

I'm relieved to hear he's not sick but confused as to why he wants to see the man who I haven't stopped hearing, or thinking, about since he returned.

"May I ask why?"

"'Cause he's cool."

"And how do you know he's cool?"

"He was in the navy and he's a doctor and he drives a kick-beep truck..." I laugh at his beep and shake my head. "...and one day, I'll own a beeping cool truck, just like him."

As soon as he mentioned Griff's truck, I should have known. Griffin owns the sweetest truck I have ever seen. It's a 1968 Ford Bronco; it's black on black and sexy as sin. It's no wonder Ollie is enamoured with Griff, or should I say his truck. My lil' man is obsessed with trucks, any and all trucks. Thankfully he can now say the word 'truck' properly. When he was three or four he struggled with that word, and it was always in a public place. One day, we were walking down Main Street and he saw a fire truck, at the top of his lungs he shouted, "Mom, look, a fire fuck." I thought Mrs. Miller was going to have a heart attack, the look on her face was priceless...the verbal lashing I got for allowing my son to use language like that was not so priceless.

I remember the first time he saw Griff's truck. He was excited. Me? Not so much. My heart froze when I saw it coming toward us. The closer the truck got, the clammier my palms became. I didn't want to see Griff, I wasn't ready to see Griff, even though it had been many years since I'd last laid eyes on him, I wasn't ready. As soon as I saw it was Mr. Steel driving, I instantly felt relieved. He parked outside the coffee shop and Ollie ran straight over to him. He managed to sweet talk Mr. Steel into letting him sit in the driver's seat. Seeing the joy on Ollie's face broke my heart, because if Griffin hadn't of enlisted and left me, this could have been what we did each and every day.

From that day on, every time we'd see that black beast, we'd have to stop and stare as it drove past, and if Ollie was quick enough, he'd get to sit in the front seat and pretend to drive. Mr. Steel always went out of his way when it came to Ollie and me. Sure, it was slightly awkward with him being Griffin's dad and all, but seeing the joy on Ollie's face, it made the awkwardness all worth it. I will do anything for my son. Anything.

"As I've told you before, Ollie, I don't think it's appropriate to just pop in to see his truck, especially while he's working. Just like we always have, if we see his truck around town, we can stop and stare." Great, now I have that OneRepublic song stuck in my head.

"Well, can we have pancakes for breakfast then?"

Shaking my head at him, I smile. I love how his little brain flits from trucks to food so quickly. "Since it's Sunday, how about we head out for breakfast?"

"Can I get a chocolate milkshake with my pancakes?"

"Only if I can get a coffee with my omelette?"

"Der," he sarcastically scoffs. "If you didn't have your morning coffee, I'd think something was wrong."

It's scary how well my son knows me, but it has been just the two of us since he was born, so it's no surprise he knows me so well. For a seven-year-old, he's pretty tuned in and as his mom, that makes me super proud.

We've placed our orders and Ollie waves to someone across the street. Looking up I see Griffin, he waves back at Ollie and then he looks at me. He winks, and I lower my head and blush.

"I like Doc Steel," Ollie says. "You should go out with him."

My head snaps toward my son. I'm shocked at what he said, but before I can ask him to clarify, our drinks arrive. As usual, Susan goes over the top with Ollie's milkshake. Even though it's breakfast time, I let him indulge. I watch Ollie devour his milkshake, and I sip on my coffee and play his comment over and over in my head.

"Ollie, baby."

"Yeah, Mom."

"Why did you say that earlier?" He looks at me,

confusion marring his chocolate-covered face. "About Griff and me."

"Who's Griff?"

"Doc Steel."

"'Cause he's beeping cool, and I like him and I like you. And like plus like equals Doc Steel."

"I don't like him," I scoff in reply.

"Yes, you do. Nana and Grumpy even say so."

"What?"

"Nana said the flame is still there. I asked her what she meant, and she said you used to date Doc Steel, and I think you should again. He's cool."

The moment is interrupted when Susan brings over our breakfast...and another milkshake for Ollie, but this time it's not as decadent.

"Thanks, Mrs. Susan," Ollie says, as he takes a huge sip of his milkshake.

Before Susan leaves, she leans down. "Ollie's right, you know." She doesn't say anything else; she just squeezes my shoulder and heads back to the counter.

As I eat my omelette, I think over everything that has happened this morning. Griffin fucking Steel is everywhere I turn...and now, he's engrained in my mind and I don't know what to do about it.

I'VE BEEN BACK FOR A WHILE NOW AND I HAVE TO say, I've settled back into civilian life much easier than I expected. It probably helps that I'm home and everyone here is known to me, but I also think my job with Doc Miller is just what I need to keep me busy.

Today I'm the on-site medic at the local ball field for the county Little League tournament. From what I've heard, it's an easy day, and an added bonus, I can check out all the hot moms—hey, I'm a guy, sue me. There's one mom who my eyes keep drifting to, and each and every time my eyes lock on hers, I see that she's staring at me too.

Game on, Autumn White, game on.

Deciding to mess with her, I stretch back. My shirt lifting to expose my stomach, my abs aren't as prominent now that I'm no longer working out each and every day, but they are still defined. I notice her inhale and I can't help but smirk.

"Put your abs away, Steel," Jamie teases as he walks over to me.

"Hey, dude, how's it going?"

"Not bad. And you?"

"Not bad," I mimic in reply.

He looks to where I'm staring. "You remember what I said?"

Nodding my head, I reply, "Yes, Daaaad." I stare at him and when he nods, I know he believes me. "Jamie, when I get my second chance, I won't be walking away from her. Ever."

"Good, 'cause I'd hate to have to kill you."

"Didn't you take an oath to protect and serve?"

"Dude, I'm a lawyer, not a police officer, but in saying that," he leans into me a whispers, "I know people, so don't fuck with her."

I laugh but from the seriousness on his face, I think he's being truthful. He leaves and I sit here and continue to stare at Autumn. She was always gorgeous, but now that we're older, she is fucking stunning. Age has done her well. Standing up, I decide to take a walk around. Of course, I strut past Autumn and her mom, Carla. I wink at her; she rolls her eyes, and shakes her head. With a final smirk, I keep walking. From the corner of my eye, I see her mom nudge her. She leans in and whispers something to Autumn and her mouth drops open. Then her eyes widen and she screams at the top of her lungs, "Ollie!" She jumps up and races over to Ollie where he's lying on the ground crying.

Sprinting toward him, I push through the kids crowding around him, "Step back, everyone," I say. "Give him room to breathe and space for me to assess him." Dropping down, I smile at him. "Hey, buddy, tell me where is hurts."

"My arm," he whimpers.

"Okay, I'm going to take a look. Is that okay?"

He nods as tears fall down his cheeks.

Resting his arm on my palm, I gently peel away his glove and have a look. From the angle of his wrist, I'd say it's broken. "Okay, buddy, looks like you've broken your wrist. I've got my truck here, so to save putting strain on the emergency services, I'll take you to the hospital myself."

He nods. "Can Mom come with me?" he sadly asks.

"Of course, buddy." I look to Autumn but she's focused on Ollie.

"Autumn," my voice snaps her attention to me. "You okay with that plan?"

"Sorry, I missed the plan."

"I'm going to take you guys to the hospital."

"No, no," she says. "We can call an ambulance."

"Autumn," Carla says, "let Doc look after you both."

I nod at her. "It's no problem, Autumn." She nods her head but she's focused on Ollie. "Autumn," I say her name louder to get her attention so she looks over at me. Her face is ashen with concern. "He'll be fine. Now, let's get him to the hospital."

She tries to stand with Ollie in her arms. Shaking my head, I stand up and bend down, taking Ollie from her, I carefully lift him up. He whimpers in pain. "Ohh, baby," Autumn cries.

"I'm fine, Mom," he says, his tough little voice wavering as we begin to walk toward my truck. Thankfully Doc Miller is here, watching his granddaughter, so he takes over as the on-site medic for me.

Thirty minutes later, Ollie is back from X-ray and Autumn is still pacing up and down the room while we wait for the results. I tried to get her to sit down, but she gave me that 'don't fuck with me' look, so I let her continue to pace.

A few moments later, the curtain is drawn back and a doctor steps in. "I'm Dr. Knight, seems our lil' slugger here has a fractured wrist." As he clips the X-ray up on to the light box, I step next to him and look at it. Then I look to Autumn, who has finally stopped pacing, "It's a clean break, Autumn, he'll be fine."

"Your husband is correct, Oliver's break is a clean one."

"He's not my dad," Ollie says.

"My mistake." He looks at me questionably.

"Doctor Griffin Steel," I say, as I stretch out my hand.

"Doctor Preston Knight, visiting from Chicago." He shakes my hand and his gaze drifts to Autumn. *Mine you asshole, back off.* I think to myself as he looks back at me and smiles. "Pleasure to meet a fellow colleague."

His name pops into my head and I realize who he is, I look to Autumn. "Seems Ollie here has the best pediatric specialist on the West Coast on his case."

"How do you know he's the best?" Autumn asks.

"Preston Knight of Western General is the best in his

field. Boston Children's Hospital wanted him to head their pediatric department, but he chose to stay at Western General and head up their pediatric department instead. It caused quite the stir when you turned down the top job in Boston."

"What can I say, I don't like to conform to what's expected of me."

"So the rumors are true then?"

He shrugs his shoulders and winks. Rumour has it, he stayed because of a relationship with a woman, who so happens to be the mom of a patient he was treating. He turns his attention to Ollie, "So, Oliver, we will get you casted up and then you can head home. I don't need to go through the instructions, as I'm sure Doc Steel here will look after you."

"We don't need Griffin's help," Autumn says. "Can you please tell me what I need to do?"

Again, his eyes flit between us. "Of course." I tune out as Preston goes over what will happen and the instructions for the next few weeks. My eyes are fixed on Autumn, she is intently listening to each and every word that comes out of Preston's mouth. Ollie is whining he won't be able to finish out the Little League season, I laugh at his facial expression. Preston finishes explaining everything, then he puts Ollie's arm in a cast—he was stoked to get blue fiberglass. Watching him work and interact with Ollie, I can see why he's the best in his field and highly sought after. I've heard stories of how amazing this guy is with kids, and seeing him with Ollie, I can see it with my own eyes. I relax a little knowing Ollie is in good hands. As a doctor it's hard to step back sometimes but knowing who is on his case, I'm happy to give him free rein to do his job without interference.

As soon as Ollie's cast has set, he's discharged and I drive Ollie and Autumn home. Ollie talks and talks the whole way to their place. No longer upset over not being able to play because he has a bright blue cast on his arm. He dozes off just before I pull into their driveway.

Carrying him inside, I carefully tuck him into bed and then walk down the hallway. Autumn is sitting on the sofa, tears in her eyes. I walk over to her. "Are you okay?"

She nods and as she does the first tear falls. Sitting next to her, I wrap my arms around her shoulder, pulling her into my side. She turns to face me and wraps her arms around my waist. She cries into my shoulder. Rubbing her back soothingly, I let her get it all out.

She pulls away from me and she lifts her gaze to mine. Our eyes are locked on one another, while something overtakes my body. Lowering my head, I press my lips gently against hers. She freezes and then I feel her tongue seeking access to my mouth. Smiling against her lips, I open up and let her in. She slides her tongue in and out of my mouth. Exploring every crevice in my mouth, she runs her fingers into my hair and grips my head, pulling me closer to her.

Threading my fingers into her hair, I gently tug the strands. She moans into my mouth, and then suddenly, her hands are on my chest and she's pushing me back. She stares at me, her eyes wide in fright. "You need to leave," she whispers.

"Autumn—"

"No, I need you to leave."

She stands up and walks to the front door, opening it up. She steps to the side and flicks her hand in a 'get the fuck out of my house' manner. Standing up, I rearrange myself and notice her eyes drop and follow my motion. Walking toward her, I stop and place a kiss on her cheek. "Call me if you need anything." I don't say anything else, I step outside and she closes the door behind me. I hear a light thud and I think she's sliding down the door; her go-to action when she's confused and/or scared.

I stare at the door for a few moments and then let out a frustrated sigh. Walking to my truck, I notice a car across the street, the driver is staring at Autumn's house. When he sees me looking at him, he quickly drives off.

Climbing into my truck, I start the engine and back out of her driveway. As I drive home, I play that kiss with Autumn over and over in my head. She feels the pull between us; I know she does. I just need to figure out how to get her to let go and give me a second chance.

Autumn and I will get our second chance, I just know it.

OH MY GOD, HE KISSED ME.

Oh My God, I kissed him back.

Oh My God, I liked him kissing me...it's just as I remembered...only better.

I run my finger over my bottom lip, it's still tingling from our amazing kiss.

Oh My God, Griffin and I kissed.

I liked him kissing me.

I want Griffin Steel to kiss me again.

No, I don't.

Yes, I do.

No-no-no, I can't like him kissing me...but it was so good.

Yes-yes-yes, I want him to kiss me again.

Oh My God, I'm so confused.

I don't know what I want anymore. I think to myself as I turn around and slide down the door. My ass hits the ground and I sit back against the door. Staring at the sofa, at the spot where five minutes ago, Griffin and I kissed. His kisses are just as amazing as I remember, if not better. My mind plays the moment over and over, and then I drift back to our first kiss when we were seventeen...

...We are in my bedroom, studying for our English test. Griffin and I have been hanging out more and more, and each time we do, the air sizzles. Our touches linger. I like Griffin, like a lot, but I'm not a hussy, so I can't make the first move. I think he likes me too, but it seems each one of us is too shy to make a move.

We are sitting on the floor, leaning against my bed. We are close together, our legs pressed against one another. I reach my hand out and pretend to scratch my thigh, grazing his leg as I do. He sucks in a breath.

Looking over at him, I see him staring intently at me. We both swallow deeply, my tongue darts out and I lick my bottom lip. He lifts his hand and with the pad of his finger, traces my lip. We begin to lean into each other. My eyes drift closed and then I feel it, his lips pressing against mine. Opening my mouth slightly, he slides his tongue into mine. My eyes pop open at the intrusion, I see his eyes are closed. Smiling against his lips, I close my eyes again and give myself over to the kiss.

All too soon, he pulls away, breaking the connection. Our eyes are locked on one another, he smiles at me and I feel it deep in my soul. I smile back, I cannot wait to kiss him again...

. . .

No, I don't want to kiss him ever again, he's the man who left me all those years ago. A noise on the other side of the door startles me, standing up, I look through the peephole but I don't see anyone there. My mind is clearly playing tricks on me, I'm obviously distracted by the fact Griffin Steel just kissed me...and it was the best kiss I've had in years.

I'm so screwed when it comes to Griffin Steel.

IT'S BEEN A WEEK SINCE OUR KISS AND EACH TIME I see Autumn now it's awkward and uneasy, not what I want for us. Only time will tell how this will play out with Autumn. I don't want to scare her, but at the same time, I want to tell her I want her. I still love her. I never stopped loving her these past twenty years. Considering her reaction after our kiss, she's not there yet. Guess I will just have to assess the situation and make my move at the right moment.

Ollie is my saving grace, he always lights up when he sees me—if only I could get his mom to light up like that around me. The lil' bugger goes out of his way to spend time with me, but I'm positive he only likes me for my truck. Hell, he can have my truck if it means by default I get to spend time with Autumn.

The last few weeks, since Ollie broke his arm, have

been pretty great; not the breaking arm part, but since his accident, I've spent quite a lot of time with them. I may be doing a few extra 'house calls' so I can check on my patient, and by default, see his mom. It's not exactly ethical, what I'm doing, but I like spending time with Autumn and Ollie.

Autumn and I haven't kissed again but she seems to be warming up to me with each visit. It won't be long before I can make my move and win back the girl of my dreams.

I'm pushing my shopping cart around the supermarket when I hear a familiar little voice. My lips lift in a smile and I quickly turn the corner, my cart bumping into another. "Shit, I'm so sorry," I say. When I look up, it's like fate intervened and I've bumped into Autumn and Ollie.

"It's fine, I should be apologizing to you. I should have been watching where I was going."

"Autumn, you can bump into me anytime." Her cheeks darken at my comment. "Ollie, my man, how's the arm?"

"Still broken," he says, his voice laced with unhappiness.

"Why the long face?"

"I can't play ball until the stupid cast comes off, and I have to have baths 'cause I can't get the dumb cast wet."

A laugh escapes and he glares at me. "It's not funny."

I look to Autumn, who is trying to hold back a laugh. "Ohh to be seven again," I say, this causes her to laugh and the sound is magical to my ears.

"You two are big meanie heads."

"I'm sorry, baby," Autumn placates him. "It's not the end of the world, you know."

"It feels like it," he huffs, then he looks to me. He has a glint in his eye that reminds me so much of Autumn when we were teenagers and she was up to something. "I know what will make this all better."

"And what's that?" Autumn asks him.

"A ride in Doc's kick-beep truck, followed by the movies where I get an ice cream and popcorn and and Sour Patch Kids aaaaand Red Vines."

I reply, "Sure." While at the same time, Autumn says, "No."

She and I stare at one another. "I really don't mind taking him for a ride, or to the movies."

"I can't ask you do to that."

"You're not asking me, I'm offering." She eyes me suspiciously. "Autumn, I really don't mind, besides, you deserve a break."

"You'll take him on your own?"

I shrug my shoulders. "Sure, why not?"

"Well, he's seven and you don't have kids...and he's seven."

"I've been to war, I'm sure I can handle a car ride and the movies with a seven-year-old."

We stare at one another again.

"Plllllleeeeeaaaaaaasssssse, Mom. Can I hang with Doc for the afternoon? Please? Please? Please?"

"Yeah, Mom, plllllleeeeeeaaaaaasssssse," I tease.

"Fine," she relents. "But you can only have popcorn and ONE other treat."

Ollie looks sad, but I lean down and whisper, "It's all good, buddy, I'll hook you up."

"No, you won't," she snaps. "I'll be the one to deal with the sugar high later." She looks to Ollie and sternly says, "One treat, mister."

"Yes, Mom," he says in a dreary, drawn out way.

"Let's go." He takes my hand, and turns to Autumn. "Bye, Mom." He drags me away, leaving my cart in the aisle and Autumn watching us as we walk away. We are outside when he looks around suspiciously and then looks up at me and whispers, "I'm not really only getting one extra treat...am I?"

"Not sure I should go against your mom's wishes, Ollie." His little face crumbles, so I drop down to his height and look around like he just did. "Buuuut there's no stopping *me* getting a few extra treats and sharing them...is there?"

"Really?" His eyes light up like the Rockefeller Center Christmas tree.

"Yeah, it will be our little secret."

"Deal." He zips his lips and pretends to throw the key away. "Let's go, I can't wait to ride in your kick-beep truck."

Three hours later, I pull into Autumn's driveway. Ollie and I stopped and got pizza for dinner, if you are having a movie and junk afternoon, you may as well wrap it up with pizza for dinner. With the box in hand, we climb out of my kick-beep truck. As we are walking up the front path, the door swings open and my mouth drops. Autumn looks beautiful in the afternoon sunlight. She's changed into a sundress that hugs her curves, showcasing her sexy as sin legs. She looks fucking stunning. "Hey, Mom, we brought dinner."

"I can see that." She lifts her gaze to mine and smiles, it shoots straight to my heart. I'd love nothing more than to slam my lips against hers, but after our last kiss, I'm not sure I want to go there just yet.

"Hey," I shyly say. "You look relaxed."

She smile brightens. "I am relaxed. I took a bath and had a few glasses of wine. I can't remember the last time I had 'me' time."

"Happy to help, Autumn, I'm here anytime you need me." She eyes me suspiciously; I see where Ollie gets that trait from. "I mean it, anytime."

"Thanks," she murmurs. "Are you staying for pizza?"

Shaking my head side to side, I answer, "No, not tonight."

"Maybe another time," she offers.

"I'd like that." Leaning in the door, I shout, "See ya, Ollie!"

"Later, Doc," comes his muffled reply, clearly he's diving into the pizza. How he can still be hungry after what he had at the movies, I will never know.

"Bye, Griff."

"Bye, Autumn."

Turning, I walk down the path. I can feel her eyes one me, I decide to be brave and I turn back to face her. "Autumn, can I take you out on a date tomorrow night?"

She stares blankly at me. She doesn't say anything. The silence is deafening. Then she nods. "I'd like that."

"Great, I'll pick you up at seven."

She nods and steps inside, closing the door behind her. Turning around, I walk back to my truck with a pep in my step and a smile on my face. This is my one chance to woo her, and I'm not going to let anything ruin this moment.

CHAPTER 10
GRIFFIN

It's 7:00 p.m. the following day and I'm standing on Autumn's front porch. I'm nervous as all hell. Taking a deep calming breath, I raise my hand and knock. It feels like an eternity until the door opens, and when it does, my jaw hits the floor. Autumn looks fucking stunning. She's wearing an orange maxi dress that makes her blue eyes pop. Her blonde hair has been straightened and on her feet are blingy sandals.

"Wow, Autumn," I say when my brain kicks into gear. "You look amazing."

"Thanks, you look pretty good yourself, Doc." I smile when she calls me Doc, up until now it's always been Griff or Griffin—I'll take that as a good sign.

"Shall we?"

"We shall." She pulls the door closed behind her and links her arm with mine...just like we used to.

Opening the door to my truck, she climbs in. Our

eyes meet and something passes between us: a pull I haven't felt in over twenty damn years. I wink at her, she rolls her eyes at me and laughs. Slamming the door shut, I walk around to the driver's side and climb in.

"So, where are we off to this evening?"

"Well, I thought we'd grab burgers at the diner to start and then if you're up for it, a round of mini-golf over in Hayden Lake."

"I haven't played mini-golf in years."

"Wanna skip burgers and go straight to the golf? We can get something to eat there."

"Yes," she eagerly shouts. "Let's do that."

Pulling out of her driveway, I jump onto the highway and head over to Hayden Lake. We arrive about fifty minutes later. Autumn jumps out of my truck, excited for the evening ahead.

We walk in and I pay for us. We grab our clubs and make our way over to the first hole. We have to wait as there's a family of five in front of us. I groan, thinking we will be waiting forever for them, my groan earns me a smack in the ribs from Autumn and a stern look. From that look, I can see why Ollie is so well-behaved, Autumn is scary when she goes all mom-zilla.

She turns to me and there's mischief in her eyes. "So, Doc, wanna place a wager on our game?"

"What did you have in mind?"

"If I win, you take Ollie for the night so I can have some me time."

"And when I win?"

She scoffs, "If you win, which is not gonna happen,

you can choose anything of your desire." Her words are laced with innuendo.

Opening my mouth to answer, she presses her finger to my lips. "Ahh Uhh," she shakes her head, "don't tell me."

"You're on," I reply, stretching out my hand to her.

We shake and she stares me in the eye. "You're going down."

Shaking my head, I laugh at her enthusiasm. Looking up, I see that the family sped through each person and we are up. Being the gentleman that I am, I let Autumn go first. She manages to get a hole-in-one, and my mouth drops in shock.

She turns to face me. "Did I not mention I'm a pro?"

"No, you failed to mention that."

"Oops, my bad," she playfully teases.

Stepping up to the tee, I take my turn and miss the hole by a hair. Walking over, I tap the ball and it goes in.

"Nice try, Doc. Seems like I'm winning."

"It's only the first hole, it's anyone's game yet."

"Yeah, it's mine," she teases. She steps up to the second hole, and just like my first shot, she misses by only a fraction. This time I manage to get a hole-in-one.

The scores go back and forth like this as we play. We throw cheap barbs at one another but most of all, we laugh and have fun; just like we used to.

We are caught up on the thirteen hole, standing next to Autumn, I brush against her arm. She shivers at the contact but at the same time, an electrical current zaps between us. The air zinging with electricity.

"So, Tiger Woods, where did you learn to play like this?"

She laughs and smiles at me. Her smile slams into my heart, leaving me feeling warm and fuzzy on the inside. "When I was at Indiana State there was one near the dorms, my friends and I used to hang there all the time."

"Sounds great. Wish I'd known this *before* I made a wager with you, but even if I lose, spending a night with Ollie is no hardship. He's a great kid."

Again she smiles. "He sure is. He's my everything." She licks her bottom lip, my eyes watch the motion and my dick twitches in my pants, and then I start imagining her lips wrapped around me. Her head bobbing up and down as it slides in and out of her mouth.

I'm snapped back to the present when she pokes me in the rib. "You're up."

Shaking my head, I walk up to the tee and hit the ball. My mind is totally not on the game and I spectacularly miss, it actually takes me four shots to sink my ball. "Naw, tough break there, maybe you should stick to saving lives."

"There's still five holes after this, I can still beat your sexy ass."

Her eyes pop open at my declaration. Walking over to her, I bend down and whisper, "Now take your shot so I can beat your sexy ass, fair and square."

She swallows deeply at my words, steps up, and takes her shot. My words must distract her because it takes her three shots to get the ball in.

We continue to dig at each other and when we reach

the last hole, Autumn and I are neck and neck. "It's all down to this last shot."

"Bring it on, navy boy," she taunts.

"You are resorting to name-calling? Are you that threatened now?"

She shrugs her shoulders at me. I step up and get ready to swing when I feel Autumn beside me, leaning into me. I can feel her warm breath on my neck, my dick pulses with want as she continues to torture me. "Hurry up and take your shot so I can beat *your* sexy ass."

Swallowing deeply, I take my shot without looking. Just like my first shot, I miss by a hair. "Naw, too bad, Doc. Let me show you how it's done."

Autumn steps up and with her eyes locked on me, she takes her shot and unbelievably, she sinks it in. She's still looking at me when she smirks and cheekily says, "I think I won."

"Seems you did."

We stare at one another, the moment is intense and then she teases, "Loser."

"Still gracious when you win, I see." We both laugh because she is far from gracious when she wins, but seeing the joy on her face right now, I'm happy to let her have her moment. We step closer together. It feels like she wants to kiss me as much as I want to kiss her. Just as I'm about to step forward, wrap my arms around her, and press my lips to hers. Someone behind us shouts, "Come on, guys, move along."

Stepping back, I bend down and pick up her ball. She links her arm with mine and we exit the course. As we are making our way back to the clubhouse, she looks up at me. There's something in her gaze. "Seems you owe me a child free night."

"Seems I do."

We stop walking and stare at one another. Just like earlier, the air around us begins to sizzle and crackle. I think she's going to lean over and kiss me, I really want her to kiss me when some kid behind us shouts, "Move out of the way." *Dammit, kiss blocked again.*

We pull apart and let the kids pass between us. Autumn purses her lips, and giggles. I love the sound of her giggle. Over the last few weeks, I have noticed she's giggling and smiling more and more...I really hope that's because of me.

The sound of kids laughing causes Autumn's smile to widen. "We should bring Ollie here, he'd love it."

"He totally would." I stare at her. "Thank you, Autumn."

"Why are you thanking me?"

"For tonight. I haven't had this much fun in years."

"Me either."

We return our clubs and as we are heading out, we decide to grab something to eat here at the putt-putt snack bar. She orders a hamburger with the works and I grab two hotdogs and fries to share. With our food in hand, we take a seat and dig in. She tells me about her life, reminiscing about her time with the guys since I left. We steer clear of the bad times she endured. The more I chat with her, the more I fall in love with her again.

We finish our meals and I drive us back to Sandpoint. Just like while we were eating, we chat and laugh. It feels just like it did twenty years ago, and all the feelings I had back then are simmering to the surface.

Pulling up outside her place, I get out and open her door. I help her out of my truck and we walk up the path. It's awkward suddenly. She unlocks the door and turns to face me, like on the path earlier, we stare at one another. I really want to kiss her, but after yesterday and her freaking out, I'll wait for her to make the move. It seems like my wish is going to come true. She leans into me and kisses me on the cheek. "Thanks for a lovely evening, Doc."

She walks inside and closes the door on me. I'm disappointed I didn't get a proper good night kiss, but all in all, this date could not have been more perfect, peck on the cheek and all.

His cheek? Why did I kiss his cheek? I wanted to kiss him like he kissed me before, but something overtook my body and I kissed his fucking cheek. "Man up, White," I tell myself, as I strip off and slip into my pale pink satin boxers and matching lace cami. Climbing into bed, I lie back and stare at the ceiling. I play the evening over and over in my head, especially when he whispered into my ear. His warm breath set my insides alight, just thinking about that moment has my clit throbbing right now.

My eyes drift closed and I slide my hand under my cami. Massaging my breast, I pinch my nipple and again my clit pulses. Sliding my other hand under the edge of my boxers, I rub my mound through the cotton of my panties. A moan slips free when I push the material aside and brush my clit with the pad of my thumb before sliding down my lips. I'm already wet and my finger slides in easily. I plunge my finger in and out, inserting another, brushing my clit with my thumb as I pull out.

Squeezing my nipple harder, I roll the taut peak between my thumb and forefinger. The sensation between my thighs intensifies, and suddenly I explode around my fingers. I mumble Griffin's name as I ride out my orgasm.

Removing my fingers from my pants, I lift them to my lips and suck off my juices. Moaning when my tangy cum hits my taste buds.

Rolling to my side, I blissfully drift off to sleep, sated and content after my amazing climax and perfect date with Griffin.

The next morning as I sip my morning coffee, I think about the events of last night. The evening with Griffin was perfect in every possible way. We laughed. We had fun...and then I ended the night with a kiss on the cheek. *What the hell, Autumn?* As I take another sip, I scold myself internally. As soon as I closed the door, I should have swung it open, jumped into his arms, and ravished him. But something held me back. There's still that lingering fear deep down he's going to leave me again.

Mom drops Ollie off just after nine and I decide to take him to the park. I need to get out of the house and keep busy...because my mind keeps drifting to a certain doctor. When I think of him, I become a horny bundle of nerves. I feel like I'm seventeen again when I think about him.

Ollie and I spent the day out, just the two of us. I think it was the first Saturday he didn't whine he couldn't play ball with his friends. And no sooner had that thought appeared, Ollie sighed. "What's up, buddy?"

"I didn't get to play ball today. Stupid arm." He shakes his cast at me, which is now a neon green color. "My life is over," he melodramatically says, and then he looks to me and there's a strange look in his eye. "You know what will make me feel better?"

This should be good. "What will make you feel better?"

"A ride in Doc's truck."

And there it is. "Well, you can't just invite yourself for a ride. That's rude."

He nods his head. "Yeah, I know. You know what else would cheer me up?"

"Knowing you, it will be food related."

His face breaks out in a grin. "Nuggets and fries and a milkshake might do the trick."

"Can we up it to cheese fries?"

His eyes widen in surprise at my reply and a grin overtakes his little face. "Yes!" he eagerly shouts. He grabs my hand and drags me toward the diner.

An hour later, we are both stuffed full. I'm glad for the walk home. Ollie and I exit the diner and we head home. We turn off Main Street and coming toward us is Griffin. Ollie immediately drops my hand and steps to the curb waving like crazy at Griffin. He pulls over and winds the window down. "Hey," he gruffly says. That one word sets my insides on fire...*I really need to get laid,* I think to myself. Then I notice Ollie and Griffin are both staring at me. "Sorry, what did you say?"

"Griffin wants to give us a lift home," Ollie eagerly tells me. "Can we, Mom?"

Looking to Griffin, I see him staring at me. His gaze is hungry, I feel it deep in my core. Nodding my head, I answer, "Sure, why not."

"Yessss." Ollie fist pumps and immediately opens the back door. He climbs into the back, leaving me to sit up front with Griffin. Once Ollie is belted in, I climb in next to Griffin. He smiles at me and I swear my panties disintegrate. Before he pulls away from the curb, he winks at me. Shaking my head, I stare out the window. Ollie and Griff talk, but I don't register anything they are saying. My mind is focused on the man behind the wheel. The more time I spend with him, the more I feel for him. He's amazing with Ollie, seeing the two of them together makes me smile. Ollie clearly likes him, since he's always talking about Doc, and if I'm honest with myself, my feelings for him are just as strong now as they were twenty years ago, well until he left that is.

We pull up to our place. Ollie climbs out and runs toward the house. Mom and Dad are on the porch. They wave at Griffin, he waves at them, and we watch as the three of them head inside. He turns his attention back to me.

Our eyes lock.

The air in the car thickens.

My heart starts racing.

We stare at one another and it hits me. I'm meant to be with him. I want to be with him. The past is meant to stay in the past, and I'm meant look toward the future; a future with Griffin.

Leaning toward him, I grip his cheeks and press my lips to his. He tenses up and I think maybe I've misread the situation, but then he kisses me back. He threads his fingers into my hair and tugs me closer to him. As our kiss deepens, I climb across and straddle him. It's tight but I don't care. All I care about right now is kissing this man.

Our kiss is interrupted when Mom knocks on the window, and we pull apart. Each of us panting. Looking out the window, I see Mom standing there. A knowing grin on her face. Griffin lowers the window. "Carla, nice to see you again."

"Nice to see you too. Ollie is going to sleep at our place tonight." She suggestively raises her eyebrows at us and adds, "Have fun, you two."

"Mom," I scoff.

She and Griffin laugh, while my cheeks darken in embarrassment. Climbing off his lap, I climb out of his truck and make my way over to Dad and Ollie. "You be a good boy for Nana and Grumpy."

"Yes, Mom." He kisses my cheek and climbs into the back of Dad's car.

"About time," Dad murmurs before he kisses me on the cheek.

"What?" I ask.

"It's about time you let him in." My eyes widen at his words. "That man still loves you, Autumn. Don't let the events of the past define your future. You deserve to be happy, and you are happiest when you're with him. Always have been; always will be. He's the yin to your yang, don't let this second chance go."

I don't get to say anything because he climbs into the

car, starts the engine, and once Mom is in her seat, they drive off. I'm left standing on the driveway, replaying Dad's words over and over in my head. Turning, I face Griffin as he walks toward me. Dad's right, I do still love him, deep down I always have. I decide here and now, to not let the past define me. I'm going to jump willingly, take a chance.

Walking toward him, I wrap my arms around his neck and press my lips to his again. He slides his arms around my waist, deepening the kiss and our connection. He taps my butt and I jump into his embrace. Wrapping my legs around him, I hold on and kiss him with everything I have.

He walks us inside with me wrapped around him. Kicking the door closed, he heads into the living room and lowers himself down onto the sofa. With our lips fused, he shuffles back and I straddle him. I continue to kiss him and shamelessly rub myself on him. All the love and feelings I had for him all those years ago come crashing back into me like a tsunami. Wave after wave of emotion smash into me, and I could not be happier than I am right in this moment.

Breaking our kiss, I stare into his eyes and it hits me, I still love Griffin Steel. Deep down in my soul, I think I have always loved him and I never stopped. "Since I feel like we should be honest, Griff, I never stopped loving you. You were my first love. You are my only love."

"I never stopped loving you either, Autumn. Being without you was hard, but it also made me into the medic I became. I threw myself into med school and the navy to keep my mind off of losing you."

He reaches up and cups my cheek. We smile at one another and at the same time, we both say, "Forever and eternity"

Slamming my lips back to his, I kiss him with everything I have, and I know this is what I want and where I need to be. Nothing and no one can take this from me.

WHEN SHE GRIPPED MY CHEEKS AND PRESSED HER lips against mine, I thought I was dreaming. Then I felt her in my lap and I knew, I wasn't dreaming. This was real.

Autumn

Is

Kissing

Me

She initiated the kiss that will be seared in my memory forever.

Carla interrupted our moment, and after saying good-bye, we went inside and here we are. She is once again straddling me, grinding herself on my cock. "Autumn," I whisper against her lips. "If you keep that up, I'm going to come."

She leans back and stares at me as she continues to

roll her hips and grind herself on me. "What, this?" she teases.

"Autumn," I growl.

She slides off my lap and sits between my legs. Her eyes are locked on me as she reaches out; flips open my button, lowers my fly, and pulls out my cock. She licks her lips before leaning forward. She grips the base of my cock and strokes. Her tongue darts out and she swipes it over the tip, licking the bead of precum. My cock twitches in her hand and she smirks at me. Opening her mouth, she swallows my dick between her lips. Sucking and licking as it slides in and out. Her eyes are boring into me, my gaze drops to her mouth and I watch as she gives me the best blow job of my life. Sooner than I'd like to admit, my balls tighten and I spill my seed down her throat. She licks and sucks every last drop.

My dick pops free from her lips, while she wipes at the corner of her mouth and dips her finger into her mouth, sucking. "Mmmmm," she moans, as she slides the tip of her finger from her mouth, down her chin, and across her collarbone. Pulling her tank down with her fingertip, she slides it between her breasts. Circling it around the crevice of her cleavage.

Leaning forward, my finger traces the path hers did. I continue down her stomach; grabbing the hem of her shirt, I lift it over her head, dropping it to the floor beside her. She's sitting on her knees, in her jeans and black satin strapless bra. "Fuck me, you are sexy as all fuck, Autumn White."

"You're mighty fine too, Commander Steel, but there's one problem."

"And what's that?" I say, as I trace my finger along her bra line, pushing the cup down I circle her nipple, gently squeezing.

"You have far too many clothes on."

"The same can be said for you," I tease, as I grab the neck of my shirt and pull it over my head, dropping it on top of Autumn's discarded tank.

Her eyes rake over my chest. She leans forward and traces her finger over my tattoo. "Vis per mare," she whispers, "What does it mean?"

"Strength from the Sea," I offer, "the motto of the ship I was stationed on."

"It's perfect for you, and exactly what I imagined you'd get."

We stare at one another again, the air around us crackling with desire. Gripping her upper arms, I pull her to me and press my lips to hers. Sliding her arms around my neck, she straddles my thighs again. My thick cock poking into her. She presses herself against my chest, deepening the connection between us. Reaching behind her, I unclasp her bra and flick it to the side. Licking down her neck, I take one of her erect pointy nipples into my mouth, gently nipping before sucking. Her head drops back and the sexiest moan erupts from her, causing her to circle her hips. My cock presses into the material of her jeans. She increases her circles, my breathing becomes labored. Her moans increase. Nipping her nipple again, her body freezes and she comes.

Her eyes pop open. Her cheeks rosy from her climax. We stare at one another. "Fuck me, Griffin," she purrs. Hopping off my lap, she removes her jeans and panties.

Shimmying mine off, I sit on her sofa in awe. Her body is just as sexy as I remember. Leaning forward, I place a kiss near her navel. Looking up at her, she rakes her fingers through my hair. Placing a knee on the sofa, she straddles me again, pressing her lips to mine once again. She pulls back and looks at me, as she hovers over my cock. I don't think my cock has ever been this hard before. She slowly lowers herself onto my shaft. Both of us moaning as the head slips into her warm wet channel. When she's fully seated, we both pause. We stare intently at one another, reaching up I cup her cheek. She nuzzles into it; turning her head she places a kiss on my palm as she begins to move her hips. Rocking up and down my cock, we gaze at one another. Resting my hands on her hips, I guide her back and forth. My hips rocking in sync with hers. She grips my shoulders and picks up speed. Our eyes are locked on one another as we give our bodies over to the pleasure building. She licks her bottom lip, it's the sexiest thing I have ever seen. Her breathing changes and I know she's close.

"Come for me, Autumn," I growl.

Her head drops back and she screams. Leaning forward, I pull a nipple into my mouth and suck as she rides out her climax. Lifting her gaze to mine, she smiles and that sends me over the edge. I come deep inside of her, gripping her hips tightly as the pleasure courses though me.

She collapses onto my chest. Wrapping my arms around her, I hold her tightly to me. Placing a kiss on the side of her head, I whisper, "I love you, Autumn."

Her head snaps up and she stares at me. Her eyes

wide as saucers. "Autumn, I never stopped loving you. Forever and eternity, that's what we always said, and it's still what I believe."

She silently stares at me. The silence is deafening and then her face breaks out into a smile. "I love you too, Griffin, forever and eternity."

She presses her lips to mine. My cock hardens between us as we continue to kiss. She lifts to her knees and lowers herself down. This is a hard and fast fuck but it's full of emotion and feelings. We come in unison, moaning each other's names.

Lifting her into my arms, I walk us into her bedroom. We shower together and then collapse into bed, exhausted and completely sated. We blissfully drift off to sleep, wrapped in each other's arms.

Waking the next morning, I'm disorientated for a moment and then the events of last night come crashing back to me. Looking to the side, I see Autumn, sound asleep. Her blonde hair, fanned out on her pillow, like a halo. She has a smile on her face and I'm sure it's a mirror image of mine. She shuffles in her sleep and the sheet moves, exposing her naked breast. Her nipples are taut and standing at attention. Pulling the sheet completely off of her, I slide between her legs. Nudging her thighs open, I flatten my tongue and lick from the bottom up to her clit. Her eyes open and she sleepily stares down at me. "Morning," I mumble against her pussy as I continue to lick up and down.

"Morning," she moans, as I slide a finger into her wet channel. "Feel free to wake me up like this anytime."

"Duly noted," I say before I dive back between her

thighs. I bring her to the cusp, and just as she's about to come, I pull away.

"Griffin," she begs but before she can complain again, I thrust my cock deep inside of her. "Griffin," she mewls as I slide in and out of her. Lowing my head to hers, I kiss her deeply. My tongue plunging in and out of her mouth in sync with my cock.

"Grrrriiiifffffffiiiiinnn," she screams, as her orgasm detonates. The clenching of her walls, sends me over the edge and I too come. Flopping to the mattress next to her, she snuggles into my side. Her fingers once again tracing across my tattoo.

Reaching down, I place my finger under her chin so she's looking at me. "Autumn, waking up next to you again is like a dream come true." I kiss her forehead. "I love you, forever and eternity."

She presses her lips to my pectoral and lifts her gaze to mine. "I love you too, Griffin, forever and eternity. And I agree, this is perfect." She pauses and swallows. "Thank you for coming back."

"No need to thank me, Autumn. I was always coming back to you, it just took longer than I expected, but you have to know; I never stopped loving you these past twenty years."

"Griffin," she blubbers.

"Shit, I didn't mean to make to cry."

"These are happy tears," she's mumbles, as her eyes continue to leak. "I can't tell you how many times I dreamed of this, and then as the years went on, I never in my wildest dreams thought it would happen." She looks up at me. "Griffin you are *the one*, my only one, and now that I have you back, I'm never letting you go."

"I'm not going anywhere this time, Autumn, unless it's with you and Ollie. You are my one and only too. Forever and eternity."

"Forever and eternity." She presses her lips to mine, and this time we make love before blissfully, drifting off to sleep wrapped in each other's arms.

***

The sound of the front door slamming snaps my eyes open. Autumn and I are still in bed. Quickly I reach down and pull the sheet up, just as I've covered us, her bedroom door opens and Ollie pokes his head in. Autumn is still asleep so I whisper, "Shhhh, Mom's sleeping."

"No, I'm not," she sleepily mumbles. "Some Heffalump slammed the front door and came barrelling down the hallway."

"Sorry, Mom," he says, as he walks to her side of the bed and sits next to her. "Are you sick, Mom?"

"No, baby, why?" she asks, her voice laced with concern.

"'Cause you're still in bed."

"Mom and I had a late night, buddy." My mind flicks to our night together and I can't help but grin. "How about you go watch some cartoons and we'll be out in a sec."

"Okay," he says and jumps off the bed and races to the living room.

"You are so good with him," Autumn states.

"He's a good kid."

"Yeah, he is," she proudly says. "Did you want to take a shower?" she offers.

"I'd love to take one with you," I confirm, as I nuzzle her neck.

"Down, boy," she teases as she pushes me away, "not while Ollie is here."

"Fine," I huff. Standing up, I walk naked toward her en suite. Turning the shower on, I realize my clothes are out in the living room. "Umm, Autumn?"

"What's up?" she says, as she steps into the bathroom pulling a sundress over her head.

"My clothes are still out there." I nod my head in the direction of the living room. "Any chance you can grab them for me?"

"Maybe I'll leave them out there and keep you here as my naked sex slave."

"No complaints from me."

"I should have known that would be your answer."

"Thought you knew me better than that."

She shrugs her shoulders at me. "They'll be on the bed when you get out."

Nodding my head, I jump into the shower and wash myself. Stepping out, I pull on my clothes, which were exactly where Autumn said they'd be. Once I'm dressed, I head out to the living room. Ollie is watching Ninja Turtles and Autumn is in the kitchen, filling the coffeepot.

Stepping behind her, I nuzzle her neck. She leans back into me, elongating it, giving me easy access to nibble. The moment is interrupted when Ollie shouts, "Can we go to the park?"

"After coffee, yes," Autumn shouts.

"Can Doc come too?"

"I'd love to, buddy."

Thirty minutes later, we all pile into my truck and I drive around the corner to the park. We could have walked the short distance, but Ollie wanted to ride in my truck, and I find it hard to say no to that kid.

We park and he runs over to the slide. Lacing my fingers with Autumn's, we walk over to a bench and sit down. She snuggles into my side and we silently watch Ollie play, the moment is perfect, absolutely perfect.

That is until I feel Autumn freeze against me. "You okay, Autumn?" I ask, looking over at her she appears spooked, and I don't like seeing her like this.

She nods. "I'm fine." She sits up and looks around, "Just thought I saw someone, but I must be hallucinating because there's no one here except the three of us." My gaze drifts to Ollie, he's now on the merry-go-round that makes me sick—yes, the big tough ex-navy doc gets queasy on a piece of children's play equipment—and he's giggling. I find myself smiling and loving the sound. There is no better sound than a child's giggle, especially Ollie's.

I get a call from Doc Miller, asking me to come to the clinic to assist him. Autumn takes that as a cue to get Ollie home. I offer them a lift but Autumn says she'd like to walk. I say my goodbyes and watch as they walk around the corner and back toward home.

Once they're out of sight, I turn toward my truck

when a guy steps in front of me, blocking my path. "Stay the fuck away," the guy growls.

"Excuse me?"

"You heard me, stay the fuck away from the kid and his mom."

"And you are?"

"Someone you don't want to mess with."

"Well clearly, you don't know who I am, because I'm someone you don't want to mess with. I don't know who you are or what your problem is, but it's YOU who needs to stay away from them."

He steps toward me, and swings. I manage to duck but his fist connects with my shoulder, it hurts like a bitch and from the force of his jab, I stumble. It knocks me off balance and I take a few steps backward. Shaking my head, I regain my balance and look up again but he's gone. I search around but no one is here. I have this weird feeling so I race to my truck, jump in and head toward Autumn's. I smile and let out the breath I was holding when I see her and Ollie on the porch. They step inside and close the door behind them.

As I drive to meet Doc Miller, I play the encounter with that guy over and over in my mind. A feeling of unease washes over me and I don't like it one bit. Who is that asshole? And why is he warning me to stay away?

IT'S THE WEDNESDAY AFTER MY AMAZING NIGHT with Griffin, and I haven't seen or heard from him since he left us at the park. I start to think maybe he regrets last weekend, but no sooner do I think that, and I receive the most beautiful sunflower bouquet from him. With this one gift, it puts all my fears aside.

On Thursday, I receive a gorgeous wine and cheese basket, and on Friday, a handwritten note. He invites me to dinner on Saturday night, just the two of us. He arranged for Ollie to stay with Mom and Dad; I totally swooned at that sweet gesture. He's amazing when it comes to Ollie and that only adds to his sexiness.

It's lunchtime Saturday and I've just waved Mom and Ollie off. He's excited to be staying the night at Nana and Grumpy's again. He's also excited for me to have my first official date with Doc. He's happy I'm seeing Griffin, well as excited as a seven-year-old can be about his mom dating.

Tonight will be the second time Griff and I will be alone since we've reunited, I'm excited because the night we spent together last weekend was beyond amazing, and I've missed seeing him this week. He has appeared in my dreams most nights, and tonight, I really hope to have a repeat performance of last weekend.

Walking into my room, I flop back onto my bed. I haven't been this happy in a very long time. I keep waiting for the proverbial shit to hit the fan, but so far nothing has cropped up. Sitting up, I look to the clock on the bedside table and see I still have a few hours before Griff picks me up. Stripping off my clothes, I walk into the bathroom. Leaning into the shower, I turn it on and let the water heat up. Facing the mirror, I smile at my reflection. There's life in my eyes again and I'm happy, over the moon happy.

Stepping into the shower, I stand under the spray and moan when the warm water hits my skin. I've been tense in the shoulders the last few days, it feels like someone has been watching me, but the tenseness could also be on account of the multiple orgasms I have been having lately. I forgot how intense and amazing sex with Griffin is. I remember to include my self-induced orgasms while thinking about the sexy as sin man and what transpired last weekend.

My eyes close and I enjoy the sensation of the droplets hitting my body. Opening my eyes, I grab my razor and shaving cream. Lifting my foot, I place it on the built-in shower bench and shave my legs and then bikini region. I actually go the full Brazilian, and I cannot wait for Griffin to feel it tonight.

Stepping under the water, I pump some bodywash into my hands and soap up my body. The water running between my thighs over my freshly shaved mound feels amazing. Sliding my hands down my stomach, I slide my fingers over the smooth skin. A moan slips through my lips when I slide the tip of my finger over my clit. My eyes close and I imagine it's Griffin's fingers sliding between my smooth lips. Dipping a finger inside, my head drops back and I continue to slide it in and out. Squeezing my breast with my other hand, I pinch my nipple between my thumb and forefinger. Thrusting another finger inside, I pump them in and out. As my breathing becomes labored, I pinch and massage my breasts as my fingers continue their assault between my legs. Suddenly, I explode, screaming into the cubicle as my orgasm detonates.

Sliding down the tiles, I sit on the floor breathing heavily. With a smile on my face, I stand up, rinse off, and climb out. Drying off, I find myself staring at my reflection in the mirror. My eyes darting between my legs, I'm not normally a fan of a fully smooth va-jay-jay, but right now, I'm kinda digging it. I cannot wait for Griff to see, and feel, it later.

There's a knock at the door and I smile. Since I'm expecting it to be Griffin, I don't check the peephole and with a smile on my face, I swing the door open. My smile instantly disappears, when I see who is standing on my front porch.

Blinking a few times, I don't believe who my eyes are locked on.

"Heya, Autumn," he sneers, a sinister smirk on his smarmy face. "Miss me?"

"Hhh...how are you here? Yyy...you should be in jail," I stammer, I can't believe Avon is standing in front of me.

"It's called parole, you stupid bitch," he snarls, anger and rage emanating from him.

I'm frozen, staring in shock at the man before me. This is just my luck, life is looking up for me and once again, I'm kicked in the va-jay-jay. I seriously must have done something horrible in a past life.

Avon slams his hand against the doorframe, bringing me back to the present. I didn't hear a word of what he said. "Avon..."

"I love when you beg my name." He licks his lips and winks at me.

A shudder racks through my body. "Why are you here?"

"I want to see my son."

"He's not your son," I spit.

"Fucking right he's my son." He turns his back on me, takes a few steps, and turns to glare at me. "Even though you are raising him to be a pansy-ass loser. You should have seen him yesterday at school, he's a little pussy." My eyes pop open when I realize he was at the school. "I should have belted you harder," he spits at me. "Thank fuck the kid doesn't have my last name."

I refuse to let him get to me, I'm stronger than I was

when I was with him. "If you don't want him or me, why are you here, Avon?"

"Because I can." His eyes roam over my body, he licks his lips again. Bile rises up the back of my throat. "You still are a sexy little thing. Are you still a promiscuous freaky bitch? Or has that navy fucker screwed you so hard, he's broken your cunt?"

I stare at him blankly as he continues to shock me with each word that comes out of his mouth. "You always were a little whore, no wonder he hooked up with you. What do you say, wanna get fucked by a real man?" He grabs his crotch and thrusts his hips toward me.

Something snaps inside of me and I move toward him, he steps back at the anger radiating from me. "Get off my property!" I shout. "You are not wanted or welcome here."

"I don't give a flying fuck what you want or what's welcome. What makes you think, after all this time, I'm going to listen to you?"

"Please, Avon. Just go."

"Not 'til I see my son."

"The son you don't want. The son who you know nothing about. The son you are glad doesn't have your last name. Why in the hell would I allow him to see you?"

"Because he's my fucking son and I want to see him," he snarls as he steps toward me, for the first time since he arrived that fear I used to feel around him starts to develop. I'm so glad Ollie isn't here right now. He hisses at me, and that's when I notice his eyes are bloodshot, his pupils are dilated, seems he's now into drugs.

"Avon, last warning before I call the police. Please

leave."

"You can't keep him from me."

"Try me," I growl at him. I don't recognize my voice as I step to him. "I'm not the meek woman I was back then. I'm stronger now, and if you try and touch me, or my son, I will fucking end you. Now get the fuck off my property."

"You're sexy when you're feisty. Let's go inside and hate fuck, that's the best kind...well, the best kind is when you tried to fight me off, but hate fucking could be like that. Whatcha say, fuck for old times' sake?"

The slamming of a car door startles me and it spooks Avon. Looking over, I see a fuming Griffin storming toward us.

"You okay, babe?" he asks, his eyes locked on Avon.

I nod my head up and down, relieved he's here. "Yeah." I turn my attention back to Avon. "Avon was just leaving."

At the mention of Avon, Griffin walks faster toward me, he places his body in front of mine and stares Avon down.

"Autumn, I will see my son, there's nothing you can do to stop me."

A sob breaks free, but before I can say anything, he storms toward his car. Griffin turns to face me and when he touches my arm, I fall apart. Dropping to my knees, I cry into my hands. Breathing becomes difficult as I process the events of the last five minutes. Managing to get my breathing under control, I look up into Griffin's eyes, currently laced with worry.

"Griffin," I whisper. "What am I going to do?"

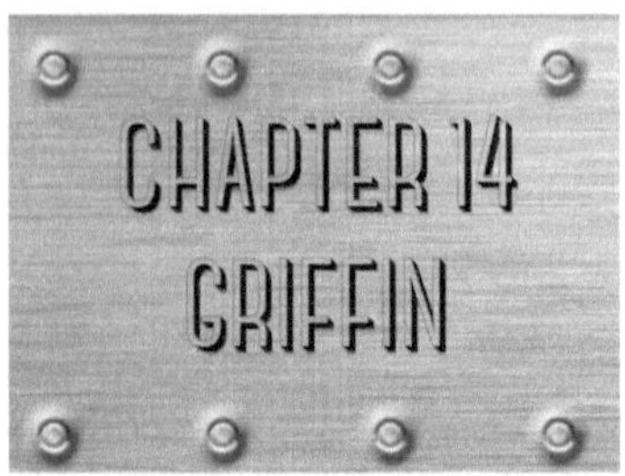

On the drive over to Autumn's for our date, I'm thrumming with nerves and excitement. I'm excited to see what happens tonight. This past week, not seeing her was tough but I get her all to myself—for the next twelve hours—thank you Carla and Howard. Pulling into her driveway, I look to her front door and smile when I see her outside to greet me, and then I see the look on her face and immediately know something is wrong. From the corner of my eye, I see someone on the path and the hairs on the back of my neck immediately prickle, it's the guy who blindsided me last weekend at the park.

Climbing out of my truck, I walk toward her. When I hear her say his name, my blood begins to boil. Stepping to her, I place myself in front of her. She's breathing deeply, I've never seen her shaken like this before. When he snarls, "Autumn, I will see my son. There's nothing you can do to stop me," a protectiveness washes over me as I turn to face her.

"I think you need to leave," I snarl between clenched teeth.

He stares at me and before I can say or do anything, he turns on his heel and leaves. We watch as his climbs into his car, tires screeching as he drives off.

She lets out a gut-wrenching wail, drops to her knees, and breaks down. She sobs like I have never seen her sob before, and we've watched *Top Gun* a million times, she loses it each and every time Goose dies. Reaching out, I rub her arm, she looks up at me and my heart breaks all over again. The real kicker is when she sadly pleads, "What am I going to do?"

Bending down, I pick her up and carry her inside. Stepping into the living room, I sit on the sofa with her across my lap. She snuggles into my neck and softly cries. "Shhhh," I whisper, "Let it all out, I won't let him hurt you or Ollie. I promise."

She lifts her gaze to mine and shakes her heads. Quietly she states, "You don't understand, Avon was far worse than I let on."

"What do you mean?" I don't like the tone she uses saying this and from the forlorn expression on her face, I'm one-hundred-percent certain, I'm not going to like what she's about to tell me.

She closes her eyes, takes a deep breath. Opening her eyes again, she stares blankly at the coffee table as she begins to speak. "Everyone thinks that last time, before I escaped, was the first time he physically assaulted me, but it wasn't." My eyes snap wide open at this admission from her. "As I've said before, he was wonderful when we first met, and he truly was. He charmed me and eventually, I fell for him: hook, line, and sinker. He was the first person I dated after you, the first person I let in, long after I graduated. I'd slept with a few others, while I was in school, but it was always just a one-night thing." I growl at this. "Down boy," she teases.

We both laugh, it is what we need to defuse the intensity in the air, that is until she continues with her story. "As I was saying, he was the first person to woo me and win my heart after you. At first, it was wonderful, and then the verbal jibes and attacks started. I put it down to stress since, he hadn't found a new job after losing his dream job after finishing college. It wasn't all the time, and he always apologized for his outbursts, and I stupidly would accept it. Finally he found a job and things between us were perfect once again. The first time he hit me, we'd just gotten home from a friend's birthday party. He accused me of flirting with my principal, who my friend was dating, and he slapped me. He immediately apologized and promised never to do it again. And he didn't, for a while at least. The slaps gradually happened more and more often. Then one weekend about a year later," she swallows deeply, "he caught up with his frat brothers and when he got home, I wouldn't sleep with him. He was wasted and that was the first time he really hit me. I ended up in the ER with a broken rib, split lip, and a fractured cheekbone." She wipes a stray tear away. "I told everyone I fell while hiking, everyone believed it due to my clumsiness. It gradually worsened after that night and he always made sure to hide the damage. He'd apologize and I foolishly fell for it each time. Two years after we started dating, I found out I was pregnant. I was scared to tell him, but it didn't matter because I lost the baby. He came home one afternoon and found me in the bathroom, blood everywhere. He was so caring and promised we'd try again. That we'd get our family and our happily ever after. He was the Avon I fell in love with again. Things between us were good, for a while after that. Just after I turned thirty, I got pregnant with Ollie. Avon was wonderful at first, but it was a rough pregnancy. I had morning sickness pretty bad so I wasn't much good to anyone. One evening, after vomiting all day, he came home drunk as a skunk and lost his shit since I was still in bed. He viciously beat me that night. I was too sick and tired to defend myself. I didn't move as he laid into me. He beat me again the next morning, just for the hell of it. I don't remember doing anything to antagonize him but then again, I never knew what I did to deserve the beatings he gave me. That day, when he went out, I made my escape. If I hadn't have been pregnant, I don't know that I would have had the courage to leave." She looks to me with tears in her eyes. "Ollie saved my life before he was even born."

"Ohh, Autumn," I sadly say, pressing a kiss to her temple, "this is all my fault."

She shakes her head. "No, Griff, no. The person at fault here is him, and him alone. And to an extent, also me."

"It is not your fault."

"Yes, it is, Griff, I stayed. I could have left the first time he hit me but *I* chose to stay. To this day, I still don't know why I did." She looks at me sadly. "Griff, I've never told anyone this. *Never. No one.* You need to keep it between us."

Nodding my head, I take her hand in mine. "My lips are sealed, Autumn. Thank you for confiding in me." I take a deep breath. "Autumn, you are stronger than you give yourself credit for. You left when you needed to. No one can take that from you." I pull her into my side and I press my lips to her temple. She rests her head on my chest. "Now, we will deal with him together and I promise I'll never leave you again."

"Forever and eternity," she quietly whispers.

I smile at her words. "Forever and eternity." As I stare down at her, all I can think is that if I hadn't of left, she never would have moved or met him. Her beautiful body and soul wouldn't have been tarnished by that monster. This is all my fault, and I will do everything in my power to protect her and Ollie from this monster; forever and eternity.

So much for our romantic dinner and night. After Avon's visit, I didn't feel like going anywhere. I changed into sweatpants and a tank while Griffin ducked out to grab Chinese and beer. We spent the night on the couch, watching *Top Gun,* drinking beer, and eating our weight in Chinese food...just like we used to. Even though it started off the way it did, it ended perfectly, wrapped in his arms in bed.

My sleep was plagued with horrible nightmares. Griffin didn't bat an eyelid. He'd hug me to his chest and whisper sweet nothings to me. Calming me down after each nightmare. As the night wore on, they became more and more vivid. At one point I woke up screaming, I was sure Avon was standing in my doorway. Griffin flicked all the lights on and checked the house.

Mom drops Ollie off around nine. They walk in with coffee and I'm on the sofa in the living room in my robe,

Mom knows something is up but she doesn't let on in front of Ollie. "Ollie, darling, can you take your bag into your room, please?"

"Sure, Nana, I'll just give Mom her coffee first." He places it on the coffee table in front of me. "Here you go, Mom?"

"Thanks, baby, I'll have it later. I don't feel like coffee right now."

He stops and stares at me. "Are you okay? You just said no to coffee."

"I...I...Griffin just made me one, baby."

"Okay," he says, shrugging his shoulders and racing off to his room.

Mom immediately walks over to me. "What's happened?"

"Mom..." I blubber, tears pour down my cheeks just as Griff walks in from the kitchen.

Mom goes into protective mode. "What have you done, Griffin Steel? Yesterday she was over the moon and today, she's a mess. I swear to God, if you have hurt my baby again, I will kill you myself. I don't care who you are."

"Mom," I whisper-yell. She turns to face me. "It's not Griffin's fault. It's...it's Avon."

Her eyes pop wide open. She doesn't say anything. She sits on the sofa next to me and pulls me into her side. Wrapping her arms around me and hugging me in the way only a mom can. "Shhhh, baby, it will all be okay. I won't let him hurt you, Ollie, or anyone."

"Moooom," Ollie shouts down the hallway.

"I'll go," Griffin says from his spot by the door. He

knows I need my mom right now. "Coming, buddy," he shouts to Ollie, as he walks past, he winks at me and heads toward Ollie's room.

"Mom, he wants to see Ollie." I start to shake my head viciously side to side, "I don't want him anywhere near my son." I lift my hands and cover my mouth. "Or me. I don't want him near anyone I love, and I really don't want him in the same fucking state as us. How is this happening? What am I going to do?"

"Autumn, we will figure this out." She squeezes my hands to reassure me. "First things first, we need to find out why he's out, and then we will make sure that the son of a bitch stays away from you both. I will not let him hurt my baby ever again. He's messing with the wrong momma bear."

"I love you, Mom."

"Love you too, baby. Now, pack a bag, you and Ollie can stay with your father and me for a few days."

"Or they can stay with me," Griffin says from the hallway.

"No, Griffin, I can't ask that of you."

"You're not asking. I'm offering." He walks over to Mom and me and sits on the coffee table in front of us. "As I've said before, him being in your life is my fault."

"Griffin Steel," Mom scoffs, "that is the dumbest thing you have ever said. For a smart man, a doctor no less, that is just nonsense. The only person to blame here is that spineless pin-dicked weasel...and now the justice system for letting him out. I'm going to have a stern word with Jamie Sherwood about this."

"Mom, why is Jamie in trouble?"

"Because, he said he'd take care of the legal things, and clearly he's dropped the ball. It must be that girl, Jenny, leading him astray. He's dropped the ball on this one and I will not stand for that, I don't care if he's my nephew."

"Mom, it's not Jamie's fault Avon was released."

"Well, I need to blame someone."

"Yeah, and that someone is the, how did you put it?"

Griffin interjects, "I believe Carla's words were spineless weasel."

"You forgot pin-dick," Mom says, this causes me to smirk. "There's the smile I love. Now, go pack a bag and head to Griffin's. Your father and I will take Ollie, so you can find out what's going on with the spineless pin-dicked weasel."

"Thanks, Mom."

"I'd do anything for you, Autumn. You are my baby girl and I will protect you until my last dying breath."

"That goes for me too," Griffin says, as he leans forward taking my hand in his and squeezing. "Why don't I take you and Ollie out for ice cream."

"It's only nine," I say, but on the inside I'm screaming, *yeah, ice cream.*

"I think you deserve a treat." He winks at me. "I'll go get Ollie."

"No," I say, standing up, "let me, but before we go, I'm going to tell him about Avon."

"Are you sure?" Carla says, her voice laced with concern.

Nodding my head. "Yeah, I am. I need to tell him so he knows to be safe and vigilant when we aren't around."

Mom and Griffin nod but regardless of that they said, I was going to tell Ollie.

Walking down the hallway, my heart rate increases. I knew one day I'd have to tell Ollie about Avon, but I was hoping he'd be older. Of course I'll gloss over certain parts, but he needs to know Avon is not a nice man and to not go anywhere with him. Stepping into his room, I freeze and scream at the scene before me.

CHAPTER 16
GRIFFIN

I'm sitting in the living room with Carla, when from down the other end of the house we hear a guttural scream. Racing down the hallway, I step into Ollie's room and see Autumn is on her knees, crying. The curtains are blowing in the breeze, the screen to Ollie's window is laying broken on his bed, and Ollie is gone.

"Where's Ollie?" I ask.

Through tears, Autumn stammers, "Aaaaa....Avon took him."

"What?" Carla questions from behind me.

"When I walked in he...he had Ollie under his arm. He glared at me and snickered before he turned and climbed out the window. I froze," she cries. "I couldn't move. I just stood here and watched as he took my little boy." She takes a deep breath. "Oh My God!" she screams. "He took my son."

Racing through Ollie's room, I jump through the

open window and into the backyard. Looking around, it's empty. A car's screeching tires from the road gets my attention. Jumping over the six-foot fence—thank you navy training—I race to the curb, but I'm too late, the street is empty and the car is nowhere in sight.

The front door flies open and Autumn comes racing out. "Where are they?" she pleads. "Ollie!" she screams. "Ollie, baby, answer Mommy. Please." She's spinning circles. She's looking up and down the street. Screaming his name over and over. I have never seen her as frightened as she is right now.

Walking over to her, I reach out and touch her shoulder. She spins toward me, her face is as white as a ghost. Her breathing is ragged; if she doesn't calm down she's going to hyperventilate. Cupping her cheeks gently, I soothe, "Autumn, look at me." She lifts her gaze. "I need you to breathe in and breathe out right now. If you keep going like this, you will collapse and then you'll be no good to Ollie." That catches her attention.

"Griff," she pleads. "I can't lose him. I can't," she says, her breathing starting to increase again.

Staring at me, I repeat over and over, "Breathe in. Breathe out." Finally she settles. "Better?"

"If Ollie was here I would be, but I'm okay...ish." She drops her gaze to the grass, lifting her head she looks to me. "Griff, what am I going to do?"

"We are going to go inside, call the police, and while you wait, I will comb the area. I won't stop looking until we find him."

Carla comes racing out, her face is ashen, just like

Autumn's. "Daddy is on his way pumpkin, as is the sheriff, James, Jamie, and Jason."

"Mom," she whimpers, she pulls away from me and walks into Carla's outstretched arms. She wraps her arms around her daughter and the two of them cry. "How is he out? What's happened?"

"We will know more when Jamie gets here." Just as she says that, Jamie and Jason pull up. Jamie is on the phone and from the look on his face he is pissed off. He hangs up. "Let's go inside," he says, and from the tone of his voice, I don't think I'm going to like what he has to say.

Everyone looks to Autumn, on autopilot she nods her head. Wrapping my arm around her shoulder, we follow everyone and I usher her inside. She takes a seat on the sofa, staring into space. My heart is breaking for her right now. I sit next to her but she doesn't register I'm here.

"What's going on, Jamie Sherwood?" Carla asks, her eyes shooting daggers at poor Jamie right now. "Why is that pin-dicked weasel out after what he did to my baby? And how in the fire-trucking hell did he get my grandson?"

"I'm still trying to find out the why to questions one and three. As for two, it seems he was released on parole two months ago. Due to a processing error, we were never advised. In saying that, he missed his last check-in with his parole officer. When he's caught, he will be thrown straight back in jail, with the additional charge of kidnapping a minor. He'll have go to trial for that. He'll be convicted and I'll make damn sure he is. I'll be pushing for maximum sentencing this time round."

"Ohh God," Autumn squeals. "He took my baby." She jumps up and heads toward the front door, she swings it open to find Howard about to open it. She looks up. "Daddy," she wails. She wraps her arms around his waist and cries into his chest. Seeing her fall apart like that is like a knife to the heart.

"...I'm not going to stop until I find out why. I will not let him roam free, even if it means—"

"Do not finish that sentence, Jamie Sherwood," Carla scolds him. "We will let the authorities do their job. I just don't understand how we didn't know he was here. Has anyone seen anything suspicious?"

That's when I remember meeting him the other day, "Ummm..." everyone turns toward me and stares. "He and I had an altercation in the park last weekend."

Autumn's eyes widen at my declaration. "What?" she screeches.

"A guy blindsided me and warned me to stay away. I didn't know who it was, not until I saw him here last night with you."

"Why didn't you say something?" she screams, she walks toward me. "Why didn't you tell me? If you had of told me, he wouldn't have taken my son." She slams her fists into my chest. "I could have protected him better." She looks up at me and out of nowhere, she slaps my face. The crack echoing through the room. Everyone goes silent, all eyes are on us. "This is on you, Griffin," she spits and storms away.

Stepping to go after her, Jamie grabs my arm and stops me. "Give her time. She's emotional and not thinking rationally."

I shake my head. "No, she's right. I should have said something. We could have prevented this." I silently add, *If I hadn't have joined the navy she never would have met him.*

"No, Griffin," Carla says, "No one could have stopped that man. I remember the look in his eyes during the trial. He's deranged. He would have gotten access somehow. It was only a matter of when. All we can do now is let the police do their job."

"Fuck that," I scoff. "I'm going to look for him."

Storming out the front door, I slam it in frustration behind me. Racing to my truck, I climb in. I need to find Ollie. I need to fix this. Once again, my actions have broken Autumn, maybe we aren't meant to get our happily ever after after all.

AFTER SLAPPING GRIFFIN, I STALKED DOWN THE hallway into Ollie's room. Pushing aside the screen, I lie on his bed and hug his pillow to my chest. His smell envelops me and I begin to cry again. He must be so scared. The look on his face as Avon jumped out the window was devastating; I never want to see a look like that on his little face again. A loud sob breaks free. "Ohh, baby, please be safe," I mumble into his pillow. Curling into a ball, I cry and cry for my little boy.

A hand touches my shoulder, startling me. Rolling over, I look into the concerned eyes of Mom. "Ohh, baby," she coos, brushing a tendril of hair off my face. She cups my cheek. "He's a tough little boy, he'll be fine."

I nod my head. "I'm so scared, Mom."

"I know, baby," she swallows. "The police are here, we need you to come out and answer a few questions."

Nodding my head, I sigh. Sitting up, I swing my legs

over the edge of the bed and rest my elbows on my knees, lowering my head to my hands. I'm exhausted but I know I need to be strong for Ollie. Looking to Mom, I sigh, "Let's do this."

Standing up, she takes my hand and together we walk down the hallway and into the dining room. Taking a seat at the table, I rest my arms on the surface and look around. I notice Griffin isn't here, and then I remember: I slapped him and said horrible things to him in the heat of the moment. "Where's Griff?"

"He's out looking for Ollie," James says, as he takes the chair next to me. He reaches over and squeezes my hand in his, just like he has many times before when it comes to Avon. That touch calms me, that is until the officer starts speaking. My heart rate accelerates and with each question he asks, all the memories of what Avon did to me come crashing back. They play over and over in my mind on a loop with the added scene of him taking Ollie. The look on Ollie's face as Avon snatched him away will be imprinted in my mind forever. It turns my stomach at the thought of what he might do to Ollie, and I race to the kitchen sink. I empty my stomach, retching and heaving. Tears pour down my cheeks as I continue to throw up. Once my stomach is empty, I slide down the cabinet door and sit on the kitchen floor and continue to cry. I can't stop the tears, the floodgates have opened and they just won't stop. James and Jason come and sit next to me. They each take a hand and hold tight. They let me get it all out. It reminds me of when Griffin left, we did this on many occasions when the grief of him leaving became too much.

Finally, the tears stop. Jason hops up and gets me a glass of water. I drink it down and hand it back to him.

"More?"

I nod, my gaze drifts to the dining room and I notice Mom and Dad are in there. Dad is sitting on the table, his arm around Mom, who has her head resting on his thigh, she staring at me. She mouths, 'I love you' and I smile. Dad rubs Mom's head and I sigh. I want Griffin to hold me like that right now, but I was a bitch and blamed him, so he left. "It's not his fault," I mumble.

"What's that?" Jason asks, as he hands me another glass of water.

"It's not Griffin's fault."

"He knows that. We all know that."

"I was horrible to him. I slapped him."

"You slapped him in the heat of the moment. He'll be fine, just like Ollie will be. They are both tough."

I nod my head but right now, I don't know if anything will ever be fine again.

The three of us stay seated on the floor, hours have passed by and there's still no word from the police or Griffin. I want to be out there looking for Ollie but, like I've been told several times, I need to be here when they find him.

The sun is starting to set and my worry is ramping up again. I'm about to tell them to fuck off and let me go search when Jamie races into the kitchen. He looks at me and declares, "Doc found him."

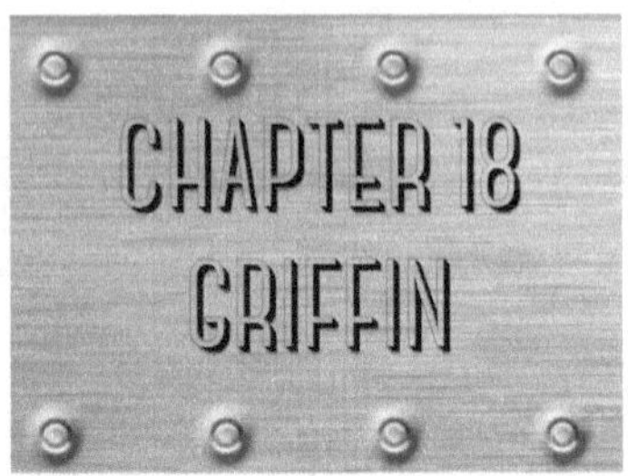

I'VE BEEN DRIVING AROUND FOR HOURS.

I feel helpless.

I'm worried for Autumn.

I'm scared for Ollie.

I'm a huge bundle of nerves...and I've been to fucking war. I'm going to lose it over a seven-year-old kid. This kid has worked his way into my heart and I would, no I will, do anything to get him back safely. I know Ollie's a tough kid, but Avon, he's a fucking psychopath. I've heard what he did to Autumn, what he *really* did to her. With knowing that, who knows what he'll do to his son.

Pulling up near the park, I need to think. My mind is racing all over the place and if I'm going to save Ollie, I need a clear head. Taking a deep breath, I hold it in my lungs until my chest hurts. Letting it out, I'm now calm. Closing my eyes, I lean my head back and think; if I were a fucking psycho dickwad, where would I hide out? Then it hits me—the lake.

Pulling out of the park, I haul ass to the lake. Around the other side of the lake, there are abandoned cabins. It would be the perfect place to hide out if you don't want to be seen. The sun is starting to set, Ollie has now been missing for almost nine hours. I will search all night; I will search for the rest of my life, if I have to. I need to find Ollie for Autumn.

I'm driving down the road that snakes alongside the lake, my eyes dart around when in the distance, I see a light illuminating a cabin on the far side of the lake. "Bingo," I say to myself, and for the first time today, I feel like I have something.

Parking my truck, I turn off the engine, switch my phone to silent, and climb out. Quietly I close the door and make my way toward the cabin. Sneaking along the shore, I start to think I should have come along the road when the door to the cabin slams open and the dickwad himself steps out. I freeze and crouch down. "Shut up, you little fucktard," he bellows, "She's raising my son to be a fucking pansy," he mumbles to himself as he lights a cigarette. He leans on the railing and I'm just about to make myself known when Ollie says something. It's muffled and I can't hear him clearly but Avon does. He growls, "For fuck's sake." Kicking the railing in anger. He throws the cigarette to the ground and heads back inside.

Sneaking back to my truck, I hide behind it and call Jamie. "Jamie, it's Griff," I whisper, "I found him. He's got Ollie in a cabin on the far side of the lake. I'm going to get him now."

"Griff, no," he says, "wait for the police."

"I'm not leaving him with that man any longer than necessary."

"Griffin," he pleads again, but I hang up on him. Slipping my phone into my pocket, I grab a baseball bat out of the bed of my truck and sneak back to the cabin. Heading along the road this time, I use the trees and shrubs for cover.

Pressing myself flat against the cabin, I can hear Ollie and Avon talking. Seems Ollie has managed to calm Avon down, it's like he knows if he keeps him distracted he'll be rescued. Popping my head up, I glance in the window and see Ollie sitting on the sofa cross-legged; Avon is sitting on a dining chair in front of him. The chair is backward and he's straddling it. He has a beer in one hand and the other is leaning on the chair back. He seems interested in what Ollie is saying. Ollie catches me and his eyes widen, Avon turns just as I duck down.

"The fuck you looking at?" Avon snarls, the way he speaks to Ollie grating on my nerves.

"A bird flew past the window. I love birds. Did you know that twenty percent of bird species migrate long distances every year? And the chicken is the most common species of bird found in the world."

"A chicken isn't a bird," Avon scoffs at him.

"Is to."

"Is not."

"Totally is. The official name for a chicken is the 'Gallus gallus domesticus' and there's more chickens on Earth than people."

"You're shitting me?"

"I beep you not," Ollie says.

"What's with all the beeping?"

"I'm not allowed to swear, so I say beep in place of the bad word."

While Ollie keeps Avon distracted with his random chicken facts, I sneak around the other side of the cabin. Climbing onto the private deck in front of the master, I spot the sliding doors that lead inside. Creeping over, I hope they're unlocked and luck is on my side. I quietly slide one open. It sounds really loud and I hold my breath, but the door to the room doesn't open. Deciding to leave it open, I sneak toward the door. I can hear them talking, Ollie is still talking about chickens. I smile. Man, I love that kid.

There's footsteps and I can't tell where they are going and then I hear the front door to the cabin open and close. I let out a sigh and quietly open the bedroom door. Peeking out, I see Ollie still sitting alone. His eyes widen when he sees me, "Doc," he whispers. Lifting my finger to my lips I mimic the 'Shhhh' motion. He nods.

My eyes dart around the room, trying to figure a way out. We need to exit through the bedroom, so I beckon Ollie to me with my finger. He nods and stands up. With his eyes glued to the front door, he walks backward toward me. "You're doing great, buddy," I whisper, "A few more steps and we can get out of here." He's almost to me when the front door swings opens and Avon steps in. He pauses midstep when he sees Ollie and me. His face morphs into anger. A force takes over my body and I step into the room, pushing Ollie behind me. I will protect him with my life.

"Was wondering when you'd show up," he sneers at me.

"Here I am." I spread my arms wide, and brazenly take a step toward him. We stare each other down, I can feel the anger and desperation coming off of him. "Let Ollie go, you can have me."

"Noooo," Ollie wails from behind me.

"Why the fuck would I want you?" he snarls, taking another step toward me. "I want the kid and Autumn."

"Not happening, Avon," I say, as I reach behind me, squeezing Ollie's arm to reassure him I'm not letting anything happen to him. Looking behind me, I want to see Ollie's okay, and in the moment that I drop my gaze, Avon lunges toward me. Pushing Ollie to the side, I take the hit from Avon. He slams my body into the wall behind me.

Ollie steps forward and grabs Avon's arm. "No, leave Doc alone," he pleads, Avon reaches out and shoves Ollie aside; he falls to the floor with a thud and shuffles into the corner.

"Ollie!" I yell. This snaps Avon's attention back to me. He swings and I duck. I swing in retaliation and my first connects with his jaw. While he's disorientated, I lower my shoulder and ram it into his stomach, sending him flying backward onto his ass.

"You'll pay for that, you fucker," he snarls.

"Bring it on," I taunt in reply. From the corner of my eye, I see blue and red lights in the distance. I need to keep Avon facing me, so he doesn't notice, but it seems my luck has run out.

"You fucking son of a bitch," he snarls, "Calling them was a big mistake."

"Letting you out was a big mistake."

"It was easy to fool those assholes. I'm reformed, blah fucking blah."

"If you give yourself up, I can help you."

"Why the fuck would you help me? You are playing daddy to my kid and you're fucking my wife."

"She was never your wife."

"But he's my fucking kid."

"So approach Autumn and ask to see him. You don't kidnap him."

"He's my son, it isn't kidnapping."

"Yeah, it is."

"What the fuck do you know, navy boy? You don't know shit." He steps toward me. "I'm going to tell you how it goes." He points at Ollie, who is once again standing behind me. "You are going to give me my son. He and I are going to walk out of here—"

"Over my dead body," I spit at him.

"Fine by me." He opens a drawer to his left and pulls out a gun. He walks toward Ollie and me, pointing the gun at my chest. His hands are shaking and I notice the safety is on, clearly he doesn't know anything about weapons. He keeps walking toward us. He's mumbling incoherently, his eyes no longer focused on Ollie and me, and I think it's now or never. Pushing Ollie in the chest, I shout, "Run!" I leap forward, taking Avon to the ground. We land with a thud and the sound of a gunshot ricochets through the cabin and then it's silent...dead silent.

JAMIE'S CAR COMES TO A STOP AND WHEN I CLIMB out, I hear a gunshot from inside the cabin. Racing to the dwelling, I push past James and Jason, who arrived a few moments before us, and barge inside. Griffin and Avon are on the ground, my eyes look around, and that's when I see Ollie, standing in the doorway to the bedroom.

"Ollie!" I shout, not caring about my safety. All I'm focusing on is getting to Ollie.

He looks up and when he sees me, his eyes well with tears, "Moooom," he wails.

We race toward one another. My arms outstretched, he jumps into my embrace. His little body heaving as adrenaline courses though him, and me. He snuggles into my chest and cries. Collapsing to the floor, we both cry in each other's arms.

A groan from next to us startles me and I notice someone pushing himself up. I panic, thinking it's Avon, but when he lifts his head, I'm met with worried hazel eyes. "Griff," I whisper, as he crawls over to Ollie and me. He wraps his arms around us, the three of us hugging each other tightly.

Hearing someone one cry out in agony causes my head to snap up. I see Jamie standing by Avon, his foot crushing Avon's hand. "Oops," he playfully says. Then there's the smack of a boot connecting with ribs. I look up to see James as he pulls back his foot and kicks Avon in the ribs, again, garnering another groan from the dickwad. "My foot slipped," James offers, just as the door swings open and officers file into the cabin.

"You good, Ollie?" Jamie asks.

He nods his head but doesn't let go of me. He's gripping me so tight, it's bordering on painful but at the moment, I don't care. I'm just happy to have him, and Griffin, in my arms again.

"Let's get out of here," Griff offers. Ollie and I nod, as he stands up and lifts Ollie from my arms. Ollie wraps his little limbs tightly around Griff's neck and torso. I stand up and wrap mine around his waist, while he pulls me into his side and presses a kiss to my temple. The three of us walk past the officers, who are now reading Avon his rights.

We walk to the edge of the porch and Griff sits down with Ollie in his lap. I take a seat beside them and rub my hand up and down Ollie's back. From behind us, I hear Avon causing a commotion. I close my eyes and then I hear the clicking sound of a Taser, followed by a loud thump.

A few moments later, Jamie, Jason, and James join us.

"Dumbfuck just got himself tasered," James says, as he sits next to me and squeezes my knee.

"He went down like a sack of shit," Jason offers.

Ollie lifts his head and he looks to Griff. "You rescued me, Doc."

"You helped me with that." He looks at Griff confused. "You distracted him and allowed me to get inside." He pauses. "Where did you learn all those bird facts?" Griff asks Ollie.

Ollie is about to answer when Avon is escorted past us and loaded into the police cruiser. My eyes are locked on the car as it drives off. Ollie's voice snaps me back to the present. "At school."

"You're a smart kid," Griff says, ruffling his hair. He stares at me over Ollie's head and winks. I know with that one wink, we will be fine.

"Thanks," Ollie says. He snuggles into Griff and then he mumbles, "I meant thanks for saving me."

"Anytime, buddy, anytime." Griffin looks to me. "Let's go home."

I nod my head and stand up. I offer my hand to Griff and he takes it. The three of us walk along the path to Griff's truck and then we drive home.

...Six weeks later

IT'S AMAZING HOW WELL KIDS REBOUND AFTER A traumatic experience. It took Autumn and me longer to get over the events of six weeks ago than it did Ollie. But together, we got through it. Ollie seems fine, not shaken at all by what Avon did, but we did make him see a counselor. She was amazed at how well he's coping, but it doesn't surprise me. He is Autumn's son and she is one tough cookie...except when it comes to spiders.

Carla and Howard are taking Ollie to dinner tonight with my dad. He is just as smitten with Ollie as the rest of us, but then again, he's been showing off my truck to the lil' guy for years now. I'm nervous, because tonight I have a question for Autumn and I'm not sure what her answer will be.

She knocks on my front door and my nerves kick in.

Dimming the lights in the living room on my way past, I take a deep breath and swing open the door. My mouth drops open and my eyes land on Autumn. She's wearing a short sundress that showcases her tits perfectly. The hem sits halfway down her thighs and on her feet are blingy sandals. My eyes drift back up to hers. "Fuck me, Autumn White, you are gorgeous."

"You're looking mighty fine tonight too, Doc Steel."

She pulls the door closed behind her as she steps inside. She rests her hands on my chest and presses her lips to mine. Pressing my body to hers, she backs into the door as I continue to fuck her mouth with my tongue. Breaking the connection, I rest my forehead against hers. "I will never get tired of kissing you."

"Me neither," she hungrily whispers, as she presses her lips to mine again.

My arm snakes around her waist and I pull her closer to me, deepening our kiss, I hold her tightly to me. With our lips fused, I walk us backward into the living room. My legs hit the edge of the sofa, spinning us around, I press her down so she's laying on the chaise. Her hair is fanned beneath her, creating a halo. "My angel," I whisper, as I lower to my knees and press my lips to her calf. Kissing my way up her leg, she moans. Her chest rapidly rising as her desire builds.

Sliding my hands up her thighs, I push her dress up to her waist, I groan when I see a wet spot on her panties. "Wet already," I murmur, as I nuzzle the silky material with my nose. Inhaling, I groan again as the smell of her arousal hits my nose. Pressing a kiss to her mound, she moans and grinds herself on my face. Pushing the soaked material to the side, I plunge my tongue between her folds. Lapping at her juices like a starved man. "Fuck, I love your pussy," I growl, as I continue to suck and devour her.

She grips my hair, shoving my face farther into her. "I'm coming," she pants, her legs gripping my head tightly as she tumbles over the edge. As the last orgasmic tremor subsides, she falls limp into the couch. Slipping her panties back into place, I pull her dress down and stare at her. "Let's eat," I say.

"I think you just did," she playfully replies, her chest still heaving from her climax.

"Best appetizer I've ever tasted," I say with a wink.

Offering her my hand, she places her palm in mine and I pull her up into a sitting position. She pulls her hand from mine and grabs my pants. Shaking my head, I stop her. "Uh uh." She pouts. "Later. Now, let's eat...food."

"Fine," she relents and stands up. Pushing on my chest, she steps past me and walks toward the dining room where I have a candlelit dinner for two set up. "Griff," she whispers, "It's beautiful."

"Not as beautiful as you," I say, wrapping my arms around her from behind, she snuggles back into my embrace. Dropping her head back onto my shoulder, I kiss and lick at her neck. She spins in my arms and presses her lips to mine. Her greedy tongue seeks access to my mouth and I willingly accept. Closing my eyes, I give myself over to Autumn and this kiss.

The timer on the oven goes off and we pull apart. "Take a seat and I'll get dinner."

She sits at the table and I walk into the kitchen. Pulling out the pot roast, I carry it over and place it between us. She grabs her rolled up napkin and when she shakes it out, something falls into her lap. She picks it up and stares at me, before lifting her gorgeous blue eyes to mine. "A key?" she questions.

Nodding my head, I grin at her, waiting to see if she catches on. "Why was there a key in my napkin?"

"Because I'm asking you and Ollie to move in with me?" Her mouth drops open, "I know it's soon but we, well I, wasted twenty years without you. I don't want to waste another second."

She stares at me. She doesn't say anything, the silence and nonanswer is killing me and then she grins at me. "Yes, Doc, yes, Ollie and I would love to move in with you. It's funny, I haven't been happy at the house since Avon took Ollie, this is the perfect solution to everything." She pushes back from the table, grips my cheeks, and presses her lips to mine. Just like every other time we kiss, it's perfect, absolutely perfect...as is the rest of the night.

Two days later, Ollie and Autumn begin to move their things in. Ollie and I are unpacking his toys when I look to him. "Ollie, buddy, I want to ask you a question."

"What's up, Doc?"

"I want to ask your mom to marry me, but I want to make sure you are okay with it first."

He stares at me, and just like when I asked Autumn to move in, it's dead quiet. He starts to vigorously nod his head. "Does that mean you'll be my dad?"

"If your mom says yes, then yes, I'll be your dad."

"I really hope she says yes."

"Me too, buddy, me too." Then it hits, I'm going to do it tonight. Why wait? We've already missed out on twenty years, I don't want to miss another moment with her, or Ollie. "Can you keep a secret, Ollie?" He nods. "I'm going to do it tonight."

"Really?" he excitedly shouts, I nod my head. "Awesome."

"Let's get this finished so I can do it."

That spurs Ollie on and in no time at all, the unpacking is finished, well his room is unpacked. The rest of the house looks like Bed, Bath and Beyond threw up. There's boxes and shit everywhere, but I wouldn't change a thing.

Now that we are done, I tell Ollie to go wash up for dinner and while he's in the shower, I'll go get Chinese for dinner. He races into the bathroom and as I watch him walk away, I realize I'm happy, deliriously happy. He pops his head back into his bedroom. "Hey, Doc?"

"Yeah, buddy?"

"I'm glad you're going to be my dad."

Before I can reply, he runs off to the shower.

Shaking my head, I walk outside and as I climb into my truck, I start to get nervous, regarding the next question I'm going to throw at Autumn.

When I return with dinner, Autumn is in the shower and when I walk into the kitchen, I see Ollie has set the table. I smile, that kid is something else. Placing a few things on the table, I return to the kitchen to grab the rest of the food when Autumn walks in.

"Something smells good," she says. Looking up, I see

she has the dress from the other night on. My cock twitches at her beauty. *Down boy.* "Wine?" she offers.

Nodding my head, I smile. "Sure why not."

"Can I have wine too?" Ollie excitedly asks.

In unison, Autumn and I say, "No."

We laugh. Ollie groans.

We all take our seats, and just like the other night, Autumn shakes her napkin. This time, rather than a key falling out, a diamond ring falls into her lap. She picks it up and her eyes are locked on the ring between her fingers. Sliding off my chair, I get down on one knee and wait for her to notice me. Finally she looks to me and gasps, covering her mouth in shock. "Autumn White, you are my everything and I thought I'd lost you, but fate bought us back together and this time, I'm not letting you go. Will you marry me?"

She stares at me blankly. Her eyes dart between the ring in her fingers and me down on bended knee. Once again, her nonanswer and silence is killing me.

"Well, Mom?" Ollie says, her eyes snap to him now. His face is etched with excitement; I don't feel his excitement and then ever so quietly, she whispers, "Yes."

"Come again?"

This time she nods her head. "Yes, Griffin Steel, yes, I'll marry you." She drops to the floor in front of me, wraps her arms around me, and presses her lips to mine. Breaking the kiss, she rests her forehead on mine, "I love you, Griff, forever and eternity."

Pulling back, I slide the ring onto her finger and bring her hand to my lips. I kiss her ring finger and whisper, "Forever and eternity."

"Yes, I'm getting a dad," Ollie proudly declares, pulling our attention to him. We both look to him and shake our heads. "Told you she'd say yes," he proudly says.

Her head snaps back to me. "You asked Ollie?"

Now it's my turn to nod. "Yep, I had to make sure the most important man in your life was happy to share you with me."

Ollie is nodding and smiling. "And Mom," Ollie adds, "he's my dad now."

Her face lights up and she presses her lips to mine again. I have never been happier than I am right now.

Time heals all wounds but love, love is the medicine that heals your soul.

...Eleven years later

THE DAY OLLIE HANDED PAPERS FOR ME TO officially adopt him was the happiest moment of my life. Then that moment was trumped when I married Autumn and she became Autumn Steel. Now today, I have a new happy moment. Today, Ollie is joining the navy and he's following in my footsteps. He's going to become a navy medic, just like me.

I've never been prouder of my son. Autumn and I never had kids of our own, but Ollie is my son in every sense of the word. Piece of paper or not, he's mine and I love him unconditionally. And then there's his mom, she was my first love. My only love. As corny as it is, she completes me. She's my other half and I cherish every day I have with her.

Sure, we had a rough road on the way to our happily

ever after. But together, we got there and became stronger along the way. Autumn and Ollie are my everything, and as I promised on our wedding day: I will do anything to protect what's mine.

Autumn and Ollie are mine, forever and eternity.

THE END!!!

Read on for a sneak peek at Falling for Dr. Kelly.

PROLOGUE

Baylor and I are lying under her bed giggling like schoolgirls. "That was awesome, BayBay. They had no idea it was me."

"I know, Avie, I know." Bay says with a smile that lights up her face. "We should do this again. It's so much fun playing each other."

"It sure is." I look to my twin sister and smile, happy that of all the people in the world I ended up with her as my twin. She's my BayBay.

"I love that you're my sister, Avie."

"And I love that you're mine too, BayBay. We are gonna be twinsies forever."

"What's a twinsie?" she asks.

"It's your twin, who is also your best friend," I explain to my older twin, by seven minutes.

"Twinsies forever," she whispers back. "Let's do it again and this time let's do it for a whole day."

"Yes, let's do it tomorrow."

As the memory fades and reality kicks back in, a sadness washes over me. Baylor and I were close and we swore we'd be twinsies forever, and up until recently, we were. She was one of my best friends, albeit selfish at times, but at the end of the day, she always had my back and I had hers. We were there for one another when we needed a shoulder to cry on or a hug just because. But she's changing before my eyes and turning into a horrible, despicable person. My BayBay, my twinsie, is wilting away and there's nothing I can do about it. This new Baylor is harsh and not a nice person to be around. She's always been the headstrong, outgoing, and brash twin, the complete opposite to me. I'm shy, quiet, and reserved. Some would say I'm a pushover but differences aside, we always had each other's back.

I want that Baylor back.

My BayBay.

I don't like this new one.

Falling for Dr. Kelly, a Falling novel is now available to buy or read as part of your Kindle Unlimited subscription.

ACKNOWLEDGMENTS

First of all, I need to thank **Kay Maree** for creating the Dirty Dozen Alpha anthology. Thanks to this anthology, Doc Steel was created. This is one of my fav stories I have written, and that's mostly due to Ollie. Man I love that kid. Without this anthology, I don't think I would have written this story as I never pictured myself writing a military doctor romance.

Thank you to my editor, **Karen** from **Barren Acres Editing;** you always have my back and I'm so glad to have you on Team DL. I cannot wait for the day we meet in person.

Thank you so much to **Stacey Blake** from **Champagne Book Designs**. I saw this cover and it screamed Griffin Steel to me so I bought it straight away. Thank you for a gorgeous cover.

As usual, a shout out to my beta babes; **Alley, Cherie, Halle** and **Jenny** . Without you guys, this would be a big old mess. Thanks for your feedback, guidance and support. Special shout out to **Alley** and **Halle** for the last minute read through after I made a few changes.

To my family, **Troy, Piper** and **Kade**; you three are my biggest supporters. Without you guys, I wouldn't be doing this. Love you guys.

And as always, last but not least, **you, my reader**. You guys are everything to me. I love the messages, the review and the general banter we have. Thank you for buying and loving my books. I hope you love this story as much as I do.

ALSO BY DL GALLIE

STAND ALONES

Out of Nowhere

Antecedent

Seven Nights

Falling for Dr. Kelly, a Falling novel

Falling for Dr. Knight, a Falling novel - preorder now

The Rule Breaker anthology

THE CASTAWAY GROVE COLLECTION

Love has arrived in the Grove

Oasis

Unequivocal Love

Five Words

...and a few more as well.

THE LIQUOR CABINET SERIES

Liquor has never been so disturbingly saucy

Malt Me (Book 1)

Tequila Healing (Book 2)

Wine Not (Book 3)

The Final Shot (Book 4)

The Liquor Cabinet: Series boxset

THE UNEXPECTED SERIES

When it comes to love, expect the unexpected

The Unexpected Gift

The Unexpected Letter

The Unexpected Package

The Unexpected Connection

ABOUT THE AUTHOR

 DL Gallie is from Queensland, Australia, but she's lived in many different places all over the world, including the UK and Canada. She currently resides in Central Queensland with her husband and two munchkins. She and her husband have been together since she was sixteen, and although they—code for me—drive each other crazy at times, she couldn't imagine her life without him.

Shortly after her son was born, DL began heavily reading again. With encouragement from her husband, she picked up the pen and started writing, and now the voices in her head won't shut up.

DL enjoys listening to music, drinking white wine in the summer, red wine in the winter, and beer all year round. She's also never been known to turn down a cocktail, especially a margarita.

www.ingramcontent.com/pod-product-compliance
Lightning Source LLC
Chambersburg PA
CBHW020229120726
47903CB00008B/2607